In His Mind, Jonathan Hazard *Was* James Bond, 007.

Licensed to kill. Suave. Debonair. Born to wear a tuxedo, and utterly irresistible to at least one woman in particular—Samantha Wainwright. She stood before him now, looking better than she had the right to.

"Is something wrong?" she asked him nervously. "I mean, I feel a little silly dressed like this."

"No," he answered. "Nothing's wrong." But *everything* was all wrong. She shouldn't be so appealing.

Perhaps she should have pulled her hair back in its usual bun. Perhaps she should have worn her glasses. Perhaps she shouldn't have applied the touch of lipstick to her mouth.

Perhaps she should have left well enough alone....

Dear Reader,

Every month we try to bring you something exciting in Silhouette Desire, and this month is no exception.

First, there's the *Man of the Month* by Jennifer Greene, which *also* is the start of a charming new miniseries by this award-winning writer. The book is *Bewitched* and the series is called JOCK'S BOYS after the delightful, meddlesome ghost of an old sea pirate.

Next, Jackie Merritt's sinfully sexy series about the Saxon Brothers continues with *Mystery Lady*. Here, brother Rush Saxon meets his match in alluring ice princess Valentine LeClaire.

Lass Small hasn't run out of Brown siblings yet! In *I'm Gonna Get You*, Tom Brown learns that you can't always get who you want when you want her....

Suzanne Simms has always been asked by her friends, "Why don't you write some funny books?" So, Suzanne decided to try and *The Brainy Beauty*—the first book in her HAZARDS, INC. series—is the fun-filled result.

And so you don't think that miniseries books are the only thing we do, look for *Rafferty's Angel* by up-and-coming writer Caroline Cross. And don't miss Donna Carlisle's *Stealing Savannah*, about a suave ex-jewel thief and the woman who's out to get him.

Sincerely,

Lucia Macro
Senior Editor

Please address questions and book requests to:
Reader Service
U.S.: P.O. Box 1325, Buffalo, NY 14269
Canadian: P.O. Box 1050, Niagara Falls, Ont. L2E 7G7

SUZANNE SIMMS
THE BRAINY BEAUTY

SILHOUETTE *Desire*®

Published by Silhouette Books

America's Publisher of Contemporary Romance

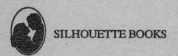 SILHOUETTE BOOKS

ISBN 0-373-05850-0

THE BRAINY BEAUTY

Copyright © 1994 by Suzanne Simmons Guntrum

Books by Suzanne Simms

Silhouette Desire

Moment in Time #9
Of Passion Born #17
A Wild, Sweet Magic #43
All Night Long #61
So Sweet a Madness #79
Only this Night #109
Dream Within a Dream #150
Nothing Ventured #258
Moment of Truth #299
Not His Wedding! #718
Not Her Wedding! #754
*The Brainy Beauty #850

*Hazards, Inc.

SUZANNE SIMMS

had her first romance novel published fourteen years ago and is "thrilled" to be writing again for Silhouette Desire. Suzanne has traveled extensively, including a memorable trip to the Philippines, which, she says, "changed my life." She also writes historical romances as Suzanne Simmons. She currently lives with her husband, her son and her cat, Merlin, in Fort Wayne, Indiana.

One

She was no dumb blonde.

She was highly intelligent, serious-minded and a brilliant Egyptologist. She was also as cold as Arctic ice—at least according to the scuttlebutt he'd heard in the hallway outside the classroom.

Not that it was any skin off his nose. He was here to meet a client. Nothing more. Nothing less.

Jonathan Hazard slipped into a seat in the last row, sat back and listened as the young female professor continued with her lecture.

"...and significant advances were made in mummification in the time period from 1550 to 1070 B.C. The techniques used to preserve the body of the pharaoh were at their zenith during the New Kingdom dynasties. The royal embalmers attempted to save everything from the king's internal organs to his fingernails.''

Jonathan held up his hands, examined the blunt-cut nails and the wide palms, then lowered them again.

"The ancient Egyptians considered the heart the center of intelligence, so it was handled with great care and stored in a separate canopic jar. The brain was regarded as useless. It was extracted through the nostrils by means of a sharp hook and discarded." He watched as the cool blonde paused and swept her gaze around the lecture hall. "I see the more squeamish of you find that distasteful."

A mind was a terrible thing to waste, thought Jonathan.

She went on in a straightforward, no-nonsense manner. "Let's not be coy. We're all adults here." Then she stopped and seemed to look straight at him, although common sense told Jonathan Hazard that was unlikely. He was only one of several hundred people in the audience. "Well, we're *nearly* all adults here." The young woman settled her long, elegant hands on her hips. He noticed there wasn't so much as a wrinkle in the skirt of her tailored suit. "No euphemisms. No cute nicknames. The Egyptians had no qualms about it, and neither will we. A leg will be called a leg, an arm an arm. Genitalia will be referred to as genitalia."

There was a twitter in the hall.

Jonathan sat up a little straighter. He'd heard it called a lot worse things.

"Contrary to popular belief, the ancient Egyptians celebrated life, not death," came the declaration. "This is evident both in their tomb art and in the wide variety of household goods buried with the mummy— food and drink, jewelry and clothing, even furniture and utensils. It was all meant to be used by the deceased in the afterlife. According to the same logic, he would also need his physical body. That is why the embalmers went to such great lengths to preserve the important parts."

Some parts were definitely more important than others, reflected Jonathan.

The professor reached for the glass of water beside the podium and took a sip before resuming her lecture. "The technique of mummifying the male genitals involved several steps, beginning with an incision that was made from the hipbone toward the pubic region."

Jonathan Hazard found himself squirming uncomfortably in his seat. He glanced around the lecture hall. Every male in attendance was doing the same. It appeared the lady had hit a nerve.

Nothing, however, was apparently going to deter her. Certainly not the minor discomfiture of any men present. "To counter the problem of severe shrinkage—" Jonathan wasn't sure he wanted to hear about shrinkage, severe or otherwise "—resin packing was introduced under the skin and molded to the original shape of the appendage. That way, when the body dried, it would retain its natural contours."

Jonathan suddenly felt like a trussed chicken. Or perhaps *stuffed capon* was the more accurate term.

He tuned back just in time to hear, ''The position of the arms in relationship to the genitals is a major factor in dating any mummy.''

He just bet it was!

As the young woman proceeded with a detailed explanation of the primary arm positions, and how embalming incisions were either pre-Tuthmose III or post-Tuthmose III, Jonathan Hazard allowed his mind to wander.

What the hell was he doing here, anyway?

But he knew the answer to his own question. He was on the job.

Reluctantly.

He was doing an old friend a favor. He had agreed to keep an eye on Professor Sam Wainwright, renowned Egyptologist, while the expert cataloged a collection of rare and valuable artifacts recently bequeathed to Chicago's Kemet Museum by an eccentric billionaire.

The task of baby-sitting a stuffy academic wasn't Jonathan's idea of a real job. He had always been a man of action, a man who had little time for the ''niceties'' and *no* time for those who lived in ivory towers. But a promise was a promise, and he had promised his old friend.

Blowing out his breath in mild exasperation, he crossed one leg over the other and plucked at a speck of lint on his suit trousers.

God knew, he had been many things in his thirty-six years: rebel, law school dropout, geologist, covert operative for a government agency he always declined to name—the average man or woman on the street had never heard of it, anyway—and now founder and part-owner of Hazards, Inc.

Times had changed since he'd hung up his trusty trench coat and put away his gun. For one thing, he was better dressed, Jonathan thought with a wry smile as he straightened his fifty-dollar designer silk tie.

He no longer wore a white hat and chased after the bad guys. He no longer knew every back alley from Moline to Timbuktu. He no longer bunked in seedy hotels, lived out of a single suitcase and ate on the run.

He had his own company, his own condo, even his own cat. He slept nights, and during the day he was usually looking after a security-conscious CEO traveling on business, or an absentminded professor about to inspect a king's—or in this case, a pharaoh's—ransom in antiquities. One thing remained constant: he always kept his promises. It was that simple.

And that complex.

Where was Professor Wainwright?

Since he'd walked in the front door of the Kemet Museum nearly a half hour ago, Jonathan had asked a dozen different people that question. He had received a dozen different answers in response. He had finally ended up here, sitting in the back row of a classroom, listening to an academic discussion of ancient Egyptian embalming techniques, and getting nowhere fast. But along the way, somebody had mentioned that if anyone knew where the professor was, the blonde would.

Jonathan decided to concentrate on the blonde.

He watched her move across the front of the lecture hall. She was attractive, he supposed, in an understated and unpresuming way. Nice voice. Nice figure. Tall. Willowy. Not flat-chested like a lot of slender women. Good legs.

Great legs.

Too bad about the hair, though. It was honey blond in color, but pulled straight back from her face into a tight, styleless bun at the nape. There wasn't a strand out of place. Not even a stray wisp to soften the effect.

She wore large tortoiseshell glasses—unfortunately he couldn't make out the color of her eyes from this distance—and a severely tailored navy blue suit. She appeared to be deadly serious. She didn't laugh, or even crack a smile. She reminded him of the old maid librarian in the small Illinois town where he had grown up.

A long and unflattering list of adjectives raced through Jonathan Hazard's mind.

Prudish.

Passionless.

Humorless.

Dried-up.

Shriveled-up.

Desiccated.

Smelling of talcum powder and musty old books, or in this case, musty old mummies.

What a pity for a young woman to be wrapped in the dead, instead of the living. The past, instead of the present. What had been, instead of what could be.

Jonathan rubbed his hand back and forth across his jaw, and swore softly under his breath. "What the lady does, or doesn't do, is none of your damn business, Hazard."

He wanted—needed—only one thing from her: information. Specifically, the whereabouts of the elusive Professor Wainwright.

"That concludes our class for today," the blonde announced in a slightly husky voice. "For further information on the subject, I recommend *Death in Ancient Egypt* by A. J. Spencer, as well as *Burial Customs of Ancient Egypt* by the museum's own Professor Sam Wainwright." There was a smattering of good-natured laughter. "The topic of next week's lecture will be Sacred Animal Cemeteries."

Without further ado, she switched off the microphone, gathered up a stack of papers—undoubtedly her lecture notes—and exited through the nearest door.

Jonathan sprang to his feet and followed.

The hallways of the Kemet Museum were crowded with students and summer tourists. Despite long years of training, he nearly lost her once or twice in the shuffle. It helped that she was tall. It helped even more that he was.

Jonathan wove in and out of the crowd, ducked down one narrow hallway after another, maneuvered around a corner and made his way through a set of imposing double doors marked Emergency Exit Only. A glimpse of a slim, shapely leg and a sensibly low-heeled navy blue pump told him his quarry was quickly disappearing *up* a flight of stairs.

He gave chase.

Taking the steps two at a time, Jonathan caught sight of her again just as the door at the end of the corridor closed. He was only seconds behind. He approached the office and read the lettering stenciled on the front of the frosted glass: Private. And under that: S. Wainwright.

So she did know the whereabouts of his client!

Jonathan raised his fist and gave a perfunctory knock. Then he turned the doorknob and entered.

The small, outer office was neat and tidy. And empty. It reminded him of the woman he was pursuing. He was willing to wager his entire fee that this was her domain: everything *had* its place and everything was predictably *in* its place. There were no surprises here.

He could see into a larger office beyond. There, chaos reigned supreme. Junk was everywhere. In fact, Jonathan Hazard didn't think he had ever seen so much stuff crammed into so little space. Artifacts covered every available surface: a bust of a long-dead Egyptian, fragments of cracked pottery, a slab of ancient stone covered with hieroglyphs, a stack of gold and silver coins, beads of colored glass and carnelian and lapis lazuli, a woven basket without a handle and a scrap of material still spread out under a microscope.

The walls were plastered with photographs and topographical maps. The desk was piled high with papers. The single window was streaked with dirt. It was impossible to tell the original color of the venetian blinds; they were a dingy gray now. There were books everywhere, some shut, some propped open.

The godawful mess must be the office of his client, the renowned Egyptologist, Sam Wainwright. Ivory towers, obviously, weren't what they used to be.

In the midst of the clutter stood the blonde in her pristine business suit. She was totally absorbed in reading the letter clasped in her hand.

Jonathan unbuttoned his jacket and nonchalantly slipped his left hand into the pocket of his trousers. He leaned back against the doorframe and began to whistle softly, randomly, between his teeth.

That brought her head up.

He flashed her his best smile and drawled in a sardonic voice, "Nice tower you've got here."

She frowned. "Tower?"

He arched one eyebrow. "Ivory tower."

She still didn't get it.

Instead, she said to him in a censorious tone, "These offices are off limits to the public."

"I know." The sign of the door had said private. It wasn't the first time he'd ignored a sign. "I'm looking for someone. I understand you might be able to help me."

Her face was completely expressionless. "I suppose that depends on who you're looking for."

He stood there. "Professor Wainwright."

Some wild hunch, some sixth sense, some gut instinct, told Jonathan what she was going to say in the split second before she said it.

The blonde opened her mouth and announced, "I'm Professor Wainwright."

Two

___

He was dressed to kill.

That was Samantha Wainwright's first impression of the man standing in the doorway of her father's office.

In fact, he looked as if he'd just stepped off the glossy oversize pages of a fashion magazine. Only, male models were traditionally effeminate young men—in reality, mere boys—and this was definitely a man.

She guessed him to be in his mid-thirties. His hair was coal black in color and cut conservatively short. There was the slightest hint of silver at the temples and crow's-feet at the corners of his eyes. His features were hard and angular, as if chiseled out of stone. His shoulders were broad; his arms long and muscular; his eyes lethal.

Something warned Samantha it wouldn't be wise to make an enemy of this man.

"*You're* Professor Wainwright?" he challenged.

She bristled. "Yes. I am."

Her unwelcome visitor showed his white teeth in a cynical smile. "Professor Sam Wainwright?"

She automatically corrected him. "Professor Samantha Wainwright."

"Then you must be his..."

"...daughter," she finished.

He thrust out his hand. Obviously he expected her to shake it. "Jonathan Hazard," he said, pumping her arm.

"I see." She didn't see, of course.

He must have sensed her hesitation. He dropped her hand, dived into the breast pocket of his jacket and emerged with a business card. He presented it to her as if it would somehow explain everything.

Samantha read aloud, "Jonathan M. Hazard. Hazards, Inc." It didn't explain a thing.

"The M stands for Michelangelo," he said with disarming charm. "My mother is an artist."

Despite her usual reticence with strangers, especially men, Samantha found herself confiding, "My father wanted to name me Nefertiti."

"After the legendary beauty who was wife and queen to the infamous King Akhenaten?"

She didn't hide her surprise. "The very one."

He was perfectly serious when he said to her, "I've been boning up on my ancient Egyptians."

Apparently so.

Samantha went on. "My mother was horrified, of course, at the prospect of her only child going through life as Nefertiti. Or Neffy. Or worse—" she made a face "—Titi. She managed to persuade my father to change his mind."

"She named you after him."

He was fast. "Yes." Samantha studied his business card. "What exactly is Hazards, Inc.?"

"My company." There was no further explanation forthcoming. "I need to speak with your father, Ms. Wainwright."

"He's not here."

She noticed he stood a little straighter. "I was told he would be."

"By whom?"

"A mutual friend."

It paid to be cautious. "A mutual friend?"

Reluctantly, it seemed, he gave her the mutual friend's name. "George Huxley."

"Uncle George," she said with genuine affection.

That brought a raised eyebrow from the man towering over her. "*Uncle* George?"

"Well, he's not my real uncle," she quickly amended. "George Huxley is a close friend of the family, and my godfather. How do you know him?"

Her visitor seemed to be choosing his words with great care. "We met some years ago under, uh...unusual and difficult circumstances."

"Unusual and difficult circumstances?" she echoed.

Jonathan Hazard nodded and admitted, "I rescued him."

She pointed her index finger at his chest. "*You* were the special agent who brought Uncle George out of Beirut?" she said, taken aback.

"I was." It was obvious he didn't want to talk about the incident. He cleared his throat and said, "Anyway, George Huxley called me several weeks ago and arranged a meeting between your father and me for three o'clock this afternoon." He glanced down at the expensive watch on his wrist. "It is now five minutes past three."

"As I told you a moment ago, Mr. Hazard, my father isn't here."

He seemed disinclined to take no for an answer. "When do you expect him back?"

Samantha told him as much as she knew. "One month. Perhaps two. It depends."

"On what?'

"The Great Sphinx."

A muscle in his face started to twitch. "The Great Sphinx?"

"The one in Egypt."

"I know where the Sphinx is, Ms. Wainwright. What about it?"

"It's crumbling."

Her uninvited guest seemed to be on the verge of losing his patience. He shifted his weight from one foot to the other and folded his arms across his chest. "It's been crumbling for centuries," he stated baldly.

"True, but the deterioration of the Sphinx has gotten worse in the past decade. My father is part of an international team of experts determined to do something about it."

"A noble endeavor, I'm sure," he said dryly.

"And a necessary one."

Jonathan Hazard unfolded his arms, ran an agitated hand through his hair and finally shrugged his shoulders. "Well, I guess that's that."

Curiosity got the better of her. "What's what?"

"If Professor Wainwright is in Egypt, he won't be needing me to accompany him to the McDonnell estate."

Samantha held her breath. "The McDonnell estate?"

The man nodded his head. "George Huxley asked me to keep an eye on your father while he cataloged the collection left to the museum."

"You're hired muscle?" she blurted out inelegantly.

His mouth thinned. "I wouldn't put it quite like that."

"How would you put it, then?"

There was an eloquent pause. "Let's just say that I agreed to be in charge of security."

Security!

Samantha saw red. It was all her father's doing. His and Uncle George's. They didn't think she could manage on her own. Well, she could. The last thing she wanted—or needed—on this project was a glorified baby-sitter.

She was as mad as a hornet. "You're supposed to act as my bodyguard?"

"Not as *your* bodyguard, Ms. Wainwright. I was asked to look after your father."

She planted her hands on her hips and glared up at the well-dressed gorilla. "Well, my father isn't here, Mr. Hazard. I am. And, for your information, *I* will be the one to examine and catalog the McDonnell collection."

Her eyes were an incredible shade of green: the color of rare emeralds.

Of course, at the moment, they were ablaze with anger. Apparently no one had seen fit to inform Samantha Wainwright of his existence.

Jonathan bit off a short expletive. The woman was going to be a royal pain in the butt, he just knew it!

"Look, lady—"

"Don't call me lady," she told him in no uncertain terms. "My name is Samantha or Ms. Wainwright or Professor Wainwright."

"Look, lady, I don't have any more to say about this than you do. The board of directors wants tight security on this job. They have no intentions of leaving it to chance, or to Archibald McDonnell's crazy heirs."

He watched as she stuck her aristocratic little nose in the air. "I can take care of myself."

Jonathan counted to ten. "Maybe you can. Maybe you can't. It's not up to me. You know as well as I do that George Huxley *is* the Kemet Museum. And frankly, whatever George wants, George gets."

She turned and said resentfully, "And Uncle George wants you?"

"He wants to make sure an extremely rare and priceless collection of Egyptian artifacts is safely accounted for until it can be transferred to the museum," he explained with far more patience than he was feeling.

"It's not fair," she protested.

"It doesn't have to be fair."

Her eyes shimmered fiercely. "I don't need your help, Mr. Hazard."

"You're going to get my help, Ms. Wainwright, whether you think you need it or not."

They'd hit an impasse.

She stared out the dirty window behind her for a moment. "I would like to speak to my godfather before this conversation goes any further."

Jonathan gestured toward the telephone half-buried under a pile of papers. "Be my guest."

She sniffed. "I'll call from my own office, if you don't mind."

"Feel free." Jonathan stepped to one side as she swept past him into the adjoining room.

Samantha Wainwright took a seat behind the desk he had known at a glance was hers. She picked up the gray, utilitarian telephone and punched in a series of numbers. He could hear it ringing on the other end.

He didn't have any choice. He was shamelessly eavesdropping.

"This is Samantha," she said into the receiver. "I'd like to speak to Uncle George, please." She listened for a moment. "I'll wait. It's important."

Jonathan waited, as well. While he waited, he studied the young woman sitting across the room from him. She appeared to be all business and no pleasure. Very prim. Very proper. He wondered if she had a boyfriend or a lover.

Or a husband?

His eyes dropped to the third finger on her left hand. No wedding band. Not that that was foolproof evidence in this day and age.

He tried to imagine what she would look like with her hair undone and clinging to her shoulders, wearing a vivid green dress that matched the color of her eyes.

He couldn't.

Jonathan decided to try a different tack. How old was she? At first glance, he had put her age at thirty. Possibly even thirty-five. But her complexion was excellent, and there was no trace of telltale lines around the eyes or the mouth. He changed his mind. Late twenties was more like it.

"Uncle George, this is Samantha. I'm fine, thank you. Yes, a letter came from Cairo today. In fact, I was reading it when a gentleman—" she paused and threw him a severely disapproving look "—when a man came into the office looking for Dad. He says his name is Jonathan Hazard and he claims to be some kind of security expert. I've told him that there's no need for his services, but..."

Jonathan watched the play of emotions wash over her face. Samantha Wainwright wasn't pleased with what she was hearing. That much was obvious.

"But..."

He could see a tinge of red creep up her neck and spread onto her cheeks. She had a lovely neck, he noticed. It was long and slender and swanlike and her skin was the color of fresh country cream.

"I'll tell him. Yes, right now." She held her hand over the mouthpiece and repeated the message. "Uncle George sends you his best. He says he's sorry about the change in plans, but my father's letter should explain everything."

Jonathan flashed her a broad grin. "Tell George I owe him *another* one."

She scowled. "Another *what?*"

"He'll understand."

She spoke into the telephone again. "Mr. Hazard says he owes you another one."

George Huxley's distinctive laughter could be clearly heard from where Jonathan stood.

Apparently the young lady had had quite enough of acting as a go-between. "Are there any other messages, Uncle George?" she inquired in a brusque tone. "Then I'll let you get back to your guests. We'll take care of business on this end. Goodbye." None too gently she hung up the receiver. Then she glared across the room at him. "It seems we will be working together on this project, Mr. Hazard. Frankly I don't like it. Not one bit," she snapped.

"So let me make this perfectly clear to you from the start. I have a job to do. I am very good at my job."

He didn't doubt that for a second.

The blonde stood up and straightened her already ramrod-straight shoulders. "For the next few weeks, I will see to my business, and I expect you to see to yours. Nothing more. Nothing less."

There was just one problem with that, Jonathan realized as he left Samantha Wainwright's private office several minutes later and retraced his steps through the Kemet Museum. She *was* his business. It was his job to keep an eye on her and the McDonnell collection. To make sure that nothing happened to either of them.

Or to Ms. Wainwright's lovely neck.

"Hey, Nick, I need you to take care of things for a few weeks," Jonathan said, sitting back in the overstuffed leather chair, drink in one hand, telephone in the other. Trigger was curled up on his lap.

"Don't worry, I'll see to your company, your condo and your cat, big brother." It was a private family joke. In truth, Nicholas Hazard was a good two inches taller than his slightly older sibling. "Hell, I'll even bring in the mail and water your plants."

Jonathan looked around the comfortable if somewhat Spartan living room with its million-dollar view of Lake Michigan. "I don't have any plants."

"Yeah, I know." Nick chuckled. "Where are you off to this time?"

"The wilds of suburban Illinois," he replied, setting his drink on the sleek Italian table at his elbow. Nick was not only his half brother, but his partner in Hazards, Inc. "It's the McDonnell case."

"Ah..." It was a very telling *ah*. "Then you're off to baby-sit the absentminded professor."

"Yes and no," said Jonathan as he reached down to scratch Trigger behind one ear.

"Yes *and* no?"

He decided he'd better explain. "Yes, I'm off to baby-sit. No, it isn't the absentminded professor."

"Who is it, then?"

"The absentminded professor's daughter."

His sibling laughed in his ear. "You're kidding?"

"Nope."

"What's she like?"

"Who?"

"The daughter, of course."

Trigger began to purr contentedly. "She's bright."

"Uh-huh."

"Blond."

"What else?" teased Nick.

Jonathan scowled. "It's not what you think, little brother. *She's* not what you think."

"Right—"

"Samantha Wainwright is highly intelligent, serious-minded and a brilliant Egyptologist," he stated.

"What color are her eyes?" came the next inquiry.

"Green."

"Gotcha!"

Jonathan Michelangelo Hazard frowned down at the streamlined black telephone he held in his hand. "What in the hell do you mean, 'gotcha'?"

Nick snorted and reminded him. "You never notice the color of a woman's eyes unless she intrigues you."

"That's pure bull," Jonathan retorted. "Trust me, this is strictly business." He had it on the best authority: Ms. Wainwright, herself.

"Sounds to me like hazardous duty," speculated Nick. "You'd better watch your back."

"Believe me, I intend to," he vowed. "I'm finished taking chances with life and limb."

"When are you leaving?" Nick asked.

"First thing in the morning. The professor is picking me up at eight sharp."

"The lady doesn't waste any time."

"No, she doesn't."

"How long do you think the job will take?"

Jonathan rubbed his chin. "One week. Maybe two."

"From what I hear, Archibald McDonnell spent his entire life buying up priceless antiquities."

"He did," Jonathan confirmed.

"How old was McDonnell when he died?"

"Ninety-one."

There was a minute of silence on the other end of the line. Then his younger brother volunteered, "Better make that three weeks."

Jonathan agreed. "Two weeks or three, I'll see you when I get back. And, Nick—"

"Yeah—"

"Thanks."

"Anytime."

They hung up.

Jonathan Hazard sat there for another half hour, content to sip his drink, scratch his cat in all the right places and watch evening descend on the city of Chicago.

Nick was wrong.

In the military, "hazardous duty" meant a high-risk assignment requiring a soldier with nerves of steel.

An image of emerald green eyes and slim, shapely ankles flashed into his mind.

Then again . . . maybe his brother was right.

Three

___

She was not a dumb blonde.

She was not a bimbo. She was not a sex object. She was not an airhead. She had spent a lifetime—well, most of her twenty-nine years, anyway—fighting the stereotype.

She *was* intelligent, serious-minded and a first-class Egyptologist, Samantha Wainwright reminded herself as she lifted her suitcase into the trunk of her car.

She just wasn't any good with men. At least not young men. Men under the age of fifty.

Men like Jonathan Hazard.

"You're the expert on the McDonnell job, Samantha," she lectured herself out loud. "You're the boss, and don't you forget it."

She wasn't about to take a back seat to anyone. Certainly not some overgrown Boy Scout. A man with more brawn than brains. A handsome ex-spy who lived in an expensive apartment overlooking Lake Michigan and dressed like a fashion plate.

Samantha wrinkled up her nose.

She didn't like overconfident men. She didn't like men who were slick and expensively dressed and who refused to play by the rules.

She didn't like men like Jonathan Hazard.

Her preference in male companionship ran to the intellectual, the scholarly, the thoughtful, the sensitive.

The boring, popped up the irreverent thought.

Samantha slammed the trunk shut and walked around to the driver's side of the vehicle. She opened the door and slipped behind the wheel. Within minutes she was in the middle of downtown Chicago, heading toward the address Jonathan Hazard had given her the afternoon before.

As long as Mr. Hazard remembered that she was in charge of this project and kept out of her way—and kept his distance—they might get along.

She snorted softly under her breath. "You've got two chances of that happening, Samantha—slim and none."

Nevertheless, she was going to be working in proximity to the man for the next several weeks. There was no getting around it. She would just have to make the best of a difficult situation.

The traffic light turned red. Samantha stepped on the brake pedal, took a moment to glance in the rearview mirror and adjust her sunglasses, then reached down to pluck a dark thread from the skirt of her tailored summer suit.

She was wearing beige this morning. She had also brought the navy blue suit she had worn yesterday, as well as one in gray, khaki, green and brown.

With matching pumps.

Shopping in quantity, Samantha had discovered early in her career, saved both time and effort. Unlike the image of the self-absorbed blonde, she had more important things on her mind than clothes. A certain uniformity made life in general—and packing in particular—easier.

Samantha was an expert packer.

She'd had to be from an early age. After the death of her mother when Samantha was only eleven, she had often accompanied her father on his trips to Egypt.

There were two rules for international travel that Professor Samuel Wainwright had applied to everyone, including his daughter. The first: she had been allowed one suitcase. The second: she had to be able to carry it herself. Her motto had quickly become "travel light."

It still was.

The letter her father had written from Cairo, dated exactly one week earlier, was neatly folded and filed in the lightweight briefcase on the seat behind her. She had read the rambling epistle a half-dozen times last night. Her father had gone on at some length about the Sphinx. And the McDonnell collection. There was one particular paragraph she recalled:

I may have forgotten to mention, my dear, that a security expert will be accompanying you to the McDonnell estate. George insists and I quite agree. It's nothing personal, Samantha, but a young woman alone, under those circumstances...

Please be gracious to him. But watch your step. Jonathan Hazard is not your ordinary man.

"You can say that again, Dad," she muttered out loud as she turned the corner onto Lake Shore Drive and looked for the address Mr. Hazard had given her.

Samantha pulled up in front of the swank building. There was a uniformed doorman standing at attention under a striped awning. Polished brass railings shone in the morning sunlight. Brightly colored potted flowers were positioned on either side of the glass double doors. She was impressed. Apparently the job of "hired muscle" paid better than she had imagined.

Before she could get out of the car, the front door of the building opened and a man emerged.

It was Jonathan Hazard.

He was dressed in well-washed jeans, a blue chambray shirt with the sleeves rolled up to the elbows and scruffy sneakers. There was a duffel bag thrown over one shoulder and a Chicago Cubs baseball cap plunked down on his head. He wore a pair of mirrored aviator sunglasses that reflected her own astonished expression back at her.

Samantha's mouth dropped open.

Where was the dapper businessman of yesterday? The one who had been dressed to kill? The one in the expensive silk tie and designer suit?

Where was the fashion plate? The elegant, mature male model?

Jonathan Hazard reached for the handle of the passenger door. "Good morning, Professor."

"What do you call *that?*" she demanded.

He followed her gaze. "Clothes?"

She snapped her mouth shut, then opened it again long enough to say, "You know what I mean."

"My disguise?" he ventured.

Jonathan Hazard tossed his duffel bag into the back and slid into the passenger seat. His legs were long. They ended up tucked up under his chin.

"There's an adjustment knob on the side if you want more room," Samantha said.

"Thanks."

Once her passenger was comfortably settled in and they were on their way, she returned to her original line of questioning. "Your disguise?"

His reply was succinct. "Yup."

"Would you care to explain?"

In a clipped, quasi-military tone he stated, "People tend to judge other people by their appearance."

"In other words, clothes *do* make the man."

"Something like that. While we aren't always what we wear, the way we look does send a definite message to others.'' Out of the corner of her eye Samantha saw him remove his baseball cap and run a hand through his short, dark hair. "Take you, for example, Professor."

She preferred he didn't.

Jonathan continued. "You're an attractive young woman, yet you choose to dress in tailored business suits that conceal rather than flatter your figure. You wear your hair pulled straight back in a severe style, and use little if no makeup. In fact, you seem to deliberately downplay your best features."

Samantha hadn't realized she was so transparent. "You're quite the amateur psychologist, aren't you?" she responded with what she hoped was a casual air.

"I have to be in my line of work."

She could feel his eyes on her. It made her uncomfortable. She found herself squirming in her seat.

He went on with his analysis. "Your appearance states loud and clear, 'There's no nonsense about me. I'm all business. I'm to be taken seriously. You're welcome to admire me for my brain, but not for my body.'"

He was right, of course, but that only made it worse. "We were speaking about *your* choice of clothing, I believe," Samantha reminded him a shade haughtily.

Her passenger glanced down at his jeans and shirt. "They give me a psychological edge."

Samantha couldn't wait to hear his explanation. "A psychological edge?"

"People underestimate anybody dressed as I am. The McDonnells are used to a horde of servants, gardeners and workmen milling about the place. They'll take one look and dismiss me as unimportant. I will become invisible. Then I can go about the business of doing my job."

"Good grief, are you always so—"

"Careful?"

"I was going to say paranoid."

"I get paid to be paranoid, as you call it," he said in a brisk tone. "I prefer to think of it as simply being prepared. That's always been my motto."

An overgrown Boy Scout, she'd just known it!

"Ninety-nine percent of the time, my job requires me to *not* be seen or heard," Jonathan told her. "I prefer to fade into the background where I can keep an eye on things."

Somehow Samantha couldn't imagine the man sitting beside her going unnoticed under any circumstances. He stuck out like a sore thumb. There was something about him. Something different. Something exciting.

Something dangerous.

She cleared her throat. "You aren't expecting any trouble on this job, are you?"

"Nope." He hesitated and then shrugged. "But trouble, Professor, often goes with the territory."

She just bet it did! "What made a man like you become a spy, anyway?"

"Would you believe I saw too many James Bond movies when I was a kid?"

"You don't give straight answers, do you?" she said with a touch of reproach.

"Habit."

"Habit?"

"In my former profession, you didn't answer any questions if you could help it. Evasive answers became a way of life, a way to stay alive, a habit."

"I see." Samantha couldn't quibble with his logic.

"The truth is I was an ordinary geologist working in a Middle Eastern country. I spoke the language. I knew the customs. I had a few friends in high places. Sometimes when I returned to the States on hiatus, interested parties would talk to me about my impressions."

Samantha kept both hands on the steering wheel. "In other words, you inadvertently fell into the spy business."

"Something like that."

Curiosity got the better of her. "What made you give it up?"

His face went hard. "I wanted my own company, my own condo, my own cat."

"Did you get all those things?"

"Yes."

Samantha knew his company was Hazards, Inc. She even knew the address of his luxury apartment. There was only one question left unanswered. "What's its name?"

"Whose?"

"Your cat's?"

"Trigger."

Maybe she had heard him wrong. "Trigger?"

"Yup."

She shot him a curious glance. "Isn't that usually the name of a horse?"

"I've always been a great fan of Westerns and cowboys, especially Roy Rogers."

That explained it, of course. "Who is looking after Trigger while you're gone?"

"My brother Nick."

"And does your brother Nick have an artist's middle name as well?"

Jonathan stretched his arm out along the back of her seat and leaned toward her with the strangest smile on his face. "You remembered."

She swallowed. "Remembered what?"

"You remembered that my mother named me after the legendary Italian painter and sculptor."

Samantha stammered. "It's n-not exactly the kind of thing you're likely to forget." She tacked on, "I've never met anyone named for Michelangelo before."

He sat back. "No."

"No?"

"No. Nick isn't named for an artist. His full name is Nicholas Longfellow Hazard. He's my half brother. Same father, different mother."

"Don't tell me. His mother is a poet."

His expression was one of surprise. "How did you know?"

"Just a lucky guess."

"Anyway, Nick and I are business partners."

"In Hazards, Inc.?"

"Yes." Apparently, Jonathan Hazard decided it was time to change the subject. "Getting first look at the McDonnell collection must be considered quite a coup in the world of Egyptology."

"It is." Samantha felt a rush of adrenaline. It was going to be the high point of her entire career.

His look quickened with interest. "What made you become an Egyptologist?"

"Everyone assumes it's because my father is *who* and *what* he is."

"Natural assumption."

She shook her head. "It's not that simple."

"It never is."

"Sam wasn't one of those pushy fathers who tried to force me to follow in his footsteps."

"Good for him."

"In fact, he tried to discourage me every step of the way."

"Why?"

Samantha took a deep breath and told him the truth. "My father thought the life of an Egyptologist was too rough, too demanding for a woman."

"You disagreed."

"Emphatically."

"You still haven't told me what made you decide to become an Egyptologist," he observed.

"When I was a girl, I often traveled to excavation sites with my father. Even now I remember the exact moment."

"The exact moment?"

"When I knew that I wanted to dedicate myself to the study of *Kemet,* the Black Land, Gift of the Nile, Egypt."

He seemed to be waiting for her to go on. Her passion for ancient pharaonic Egypt wasn't something she usually talked about to outsiders—most people were bored stiff by the subject—but Jonathan Hazard appeared genuinely interested.

So Samantha told him, unaware that her voice took on a reverence in the process. "We were in the Valley of the Queens. I was alone for a few minutes. I entered the tomb of Nefetari, wife of the great pharaoh Merneptah Seti, more commonly known as Seti III. And there, on the walls of her burial chamber, the colors still as vivid and vibrant as the day it was painted, was a portrait of the queen. She was reading a papyrus. It was a love poem written to her by her husband."

"How extraordinary," muttered the man beside her.

Samantha felt a chill course down her spine as she recited the poem long ago committed to memory:

Hail to thee, Nefetari, most beauteous of women,
Consort of the God, beloved of Him who wears
      the two crowns,
Thou art fair in face, graced with a body and
      spirit that is perfection.
Isis incarnate, how the Gods worship thee!
Thy breasts are sweeter than honey,
Thy beauty greater than the fabled Nefetiri,
Thy skin finer than the gold of Kush,

Thy eyes darkest ebony.
Thy voice is more pleasing than the music of the
          harp, than the sound of the River of Life
          at dawn.
Thou art favored by the Gods.
They call thee by name and it is Egypt.
And when They see thee come, it is said, the
     ·   Beautiful One comes!

"The eternal landscape of Egypt—its past, present and future—they are as one." Her voice was hushed and filled with awe. "That was the exact moment I knew."

He took it back.

He took it all back. Every last word. Samantha Wainwright was not prudish. She was not passionless. She was not dried-up nor shriveled-up.

She was a woman capable of great passion, of grand passion, whether she knew it or not. She was a creature of the senses. She was emotional. She was dramatic. And she was, at heart, a romantic.

Jonathan was enthralled and utterly fascinated. Samantha was not at all the woman she had seemed to be.

A scowl creased his forehead. He had made a grave tactical error. He had underestimated the enemy, something he would not have done a year or two ago.

"I apologize for getting carried away like that," she said a bit sheepishly as she turned off the expressway and drove into the countryside. "I think we should discuss some practical matters before we reach Fontainebleau."

"Fontainebleau?" He was still thinking about the startling revelation that Professor Wainwright was all woman through and through.

She gave him a quick sideways glance. "Archibald McDonnell's estate."

"Oh, *that* Fontainebleau," he said, slapping his forehead with the brim of his Cubs hat.

"Yes, *that* Fontainebleau."

"I believe it's a replica of the original palace in France," he said conversationally. "It was from Fontainebleau's horseshoe-shaped staircase that Napoleon bade farewell to the Imperial Guard in the spring of 1814."

"Been boning up on your French history, as well?"

Jonathan grinned at her. "Just gathering a little background information. I never like to go into any situation blind." In the old days, it had often meant the difference between life and death. Old habits, he had found, died hard. "What do you know about Archibald McDonnell?"

She chewed on her bottom lip as she mulled it over, then replied, "Archibald McDonnell was a self-made billionaire. He was brilliant, eccentric, somewhat paranoid, and a devout, lifelong bachelor. He was also a passionate student of history and a compulsive collector of antiquities. He had the money to indulge himself, and he did. His collections, only one of which is Egyptian, have been the subject of speculation for decades. He apparently decided to bequeath his

Egyptian artifacts to the Kemet Museum because of his admiration and respect for George Huxley.''

"I see you've been boning up on McDonnell.''

"Under the circumstances, it seemed like the reasonable thing to do.''

"What do you know of the heirs?'' he grilled.

"Not much.'' She wet her lips with the tip of her tongue. "I believe the primary heirs are a great-nephew and his wife.''

Jonathan nodded and filled her in. "The nephew's name is Henry McDonnell. His wife is Carlotta. They are both in their fifties and a bit odd.''

"Somehow I'm not surprised.''

"Henry bought himself a title while he was in Paris several years ago and now insists upon being addressed as Prince Henri.'' He watched as Samantha raised a dark blond eyebrow over the rim of her sunglasses. "My sentiments precisely. Henry speaks atrocious French, by the way.''

He could hear the astonishment in her voice. "How in the world did you find out something like that?''

"I have my ways.''

"Keep a few contacts from your spy days, do you?''

His sources were private, secret, sacrosanct. "Anyway, Carlotta—''

"Not Princess Carlotta?'' she interjected.

He shook his head. "His wife goes simply by Carlotta to her friends, Madam to the servants and Mrs. McDonnell to the rest of us. Nevertheless, Carlotta has her own little idiosyncrasies.''

"What are they?''

He was succinct. "Hats."

Samantha Wainwright puckered her forehead. "Hats?"

"Hats. Bonnets. Headgear. Chapeaus."

"I fail to see what is so strange about hats."

"Carlotta always wears a hat, no matter what the occasion. Day or night. Summer, winter, spring or fall."

"And—?"

"And she is purported to change her hat four and five times a day."

Her mouth formed an O.

"Carlotta owns three thousand hats."

"Oh, dear..."

"Carlotta McDonnell also collects Pekingese."

This time Samantha Wainwright brought the automobile to a dead stop, removed her sunglasses and looked him straight in the eyes. "Pekingese? As in the small, short-legged, long-haired, yappy little dog?"

"Yes."

She slipped her sunglasses back into place, put the car in gear, pressed on the gas pedal and continued driving along the country road. "I'm almost afraid to ask how many Pekingese our hostess has managed to accumulate."

"At last count, fourteen. But only six are allowed to share her boudoir at any given time. Apparently, some kind of rotation system has been set up."

"Dogs." She made a face that clearly expressed her opinion of man's supposed best friend. "I've always preferred cats, myself."

"Trigger will be gratified to hear that."

Samantha turned off the country road and stopped in front of a huge wrought-iron gate. In the center was a gigantic and ornate letter F formed by the grillwork. To either side of the gate was a ten-foot-high stone wall. "Well, here we are," she announced. "Fontainebleau."

"All I see is a gate and a wall."

"The McDonnells are very private people."

Jonathan watched as Samantha rolled down her window, reached out and pushed a button beneath an intercom system.

It was several minutes before a disembodied voice inquired, "State your name and business, please."

"Professor Samantha Wainwright. I'm here in my official capacity with the Kemet Museum."

"Of course, Professor. We have been expecting you. Please proceed through the gate, which is now opening, and along the main road until you reach the front entrance. And welcome to Fontainebleau."

The gate slowly swung open and Samantha Wainwright drove through.

"By the way," Jonathan felt compelled to quickly add, "I should mention that there is a man named Crispy Green in residence, as well as a very proper British butler, and a housekeeper named Mrs. Danvers."

A low groan issued forth from his companion.

He frowned. "What's wrong?"

"Didn't you ever read Daphne Du Maurier's *Rebecca?*"

"I'm afraid not."

"Well, there was an evil and foreboding house-keeper in the book named Mrs. Danvers. It wasn't a case of the butler doing it, but the housekeeper."

"Doing *what?*"

"Murder. Or attempted murder, anyway. Mrs. Danvers tried to do away with her new mistress by driving the poor creature to suicide. In the end, of course, it was the housekeeper who went up in smoke with Manderley."

"Manderley?"

"The house." Samantha gnawed on her bottom lip again. "More like a castle, really. It burned to the ground."

Jonathan didn't mind admitting he was confused. But before he could ask any more questions, they came around a bend in the road and there, in the distance, sitting majestically on a rise of green rolling lawns, was Fontainebleau.

"Well, I never!" exclaimed Samantha.

Somehow *that* didn't surprise Jonathan.

He took off his aviator glasses and stared at the great stone castle. "I guess Archibald McDonnell literally believed in the old adage."

"What old adage?" she asked.

"That a man's home is his castle."

Four

"**P**rofessor Wainwright, I presume," greeted the very proper British butler who opened the front door.

"You presume correctly," Samantha assured the immaculate man in the immaculate dark suit.

"Welcome to Fontainebleau, Professor."

"Thank you."

He gave Samantha a polite nod. "The name is Trout."

"Thank you, Trout."

He glanced over her left shoulder at Jonathan Hazard. "And this must be..."

Samantha's mind went blank. She blinked once, twice, three times in quick succession. She hadn't thought to ask the blasted Boy Scout what his cover was going to be. Now what was she supposed to do?

Stick to the simple truth, Samantha.

With a small flourish of her hand, she said, "This is Jonathan Hazard."

Trout looked down his considerable nose at her companion. "Mr. Hazard."

Out of the corner of her eye, she saw Jonathan acknowledge the other man with equanimity. "Trout."

The butler's attention reverted to her. "And Mr. Hazard is..."

"Mr. Hazard is my..."

Assistant?

Samantha didn't think anyone would believe that Jonathan Hazard was a fellow Egyptologist.

Bodyguard?

Jonathan claimed that he wasn't her bodyguard, that he was simply in charge of security.

Hired muscle?

Glorified baby-sitter?

Both were true, but she could scarcely imagine herself blurting out either one to the dignified Englishman.

Trout attempted to smooth over the awkward moment. "Your gentleman friend?"

Samantha choked on her saliva.

Before she could correct the outrageous suggestion, Jonathan took a step toward her and slipped a possessive—and familiar—arm around her waist. "That's right, Trout. I'm the professor's gentleman friend." He looked down at her and grinned. "Isn't that so, Sam, honey?"

Sam, honey?

Samantha saw red. Bright red. Bloodred. She wanted to spit in his eye and call him a liar. She wanted to kick him in the shins. Hard. She wanted to do whatever it took to wipe the stupid grin off Jonathan Hazard's handsome face.

And he knew it.

They both also knew if she contradicted him now, she would look pretty ridiculous. She would have to wait and take the matter up with Mr. Hazard in private.

Samantha gritted her teeth. "Yes, Jonathan, *dear?*"

Trout took it all in his stride. "If I may have the keys to your automobile, Professor, I will arrange for your luggage to be taken to your rooms."

She handed over her key chain. "Thank you, Trout."

"Perhaps you would like to freshen up before luncheon. You will be on your own, I'm afraid. It was requested that I extend abject apologies on behalf of the prince and Madam. They are otherwise engaged. They will, however, see you at dinner."

"That's quite all right. We don't expect to be treated like honored guests," Samantha told him. "After all, I'm here to do a job."

"Indeed, Professor Wainwright, I understand that you are a world-renowned Egyptologist." Trout gestured toward the grand staircase. "You will find that your rooms are, appropriately, located in the Egyptian wing of the house."

Samantha felt a rush of excitement at the thought of the treasures she would soon be seeing for the first time. "The McDonnell collection is certainly world-renowned."

Trout seemed to take her comment as a personal compliment. There was the slightest hint of a smile on his otherwise stoic features when he announced, "Martin will escort you upstairs."

Without so much as a snap of Trout's fingers, a slightly younger man appeared at the butler's side. "Yes, Mr. Trout," he said with due respect.

"Would you show Professor Wainwright and Mr. Hazard to their rooms in the Egyptian wing?"

"Of course, Mr. Trout." Martin turned to them. "If you will follow me, please."

Martin led the way across the marble foyer and up the sweeping staircase. He indicated the massive chandelier suspended from the three-story-high ceiling. "It may be of interest to note that this is one of the largest crystal chandeliers in existence in a private home. The chandelier was commissioned by Mr. McDonnell for the entrance hall in 1952."

"Very impressive," murmured Samantha.

"It takes a staff of four an entire day to clean and change the one thousand light bulbs in the chandelier," Martin said without joy.

"A daunting task, I'm sure," remarked Jonathan.

Martin obviously relished having a captive audience. "Fontainebleau is a famous château in France. Construction of the original was begun in approximately 1137, during the reign of Louis VI the Fat. It was initially used as a hunting lodge. The present palace, which served as a model for this house, was built in the sixteenth century and was utilized at one time by the Emperor Napoléon.''

Jonathan lowered his voice and griped, ''He sounds like a travel guide.''

Samantha gave him a dirty look. She gave Martin a smile of encouragement. ''Fascinating.''

They traipsed along behind the footman until they reached the top of the staircase. Here they encountered vast display cases lined up all along the far wall.

''Mr. McDonnell also acquired in his lifetime one of the largest collections of early eighteenth-century Meissen porcelain in the world, including the most famous of the large dinner services, the 'Swan.''' Next, the young man made a gesture toward a row of windows. ''You may wish to stop and admire the lovely view of the rose garden, the park and Lake McDonnell from this vantage point.''

''I knew it, it's the bloody house-and-garden tour,'' Jonathan muttered under his breath.

Samantha ignored him. She gazed out one of the windows for a minute or two and made the appropriate noises of appreciation to the footman. Then they proceeded into the Egyptian wing of the vast house.

''This is...'' Samantha found herself at a loss for words.

''You can say that again,'' Jonathan piped up.

''Impressive? Splendid? Magnificent?'' Martin volunteered. ''It is all of these things and more. A dozen artisans labored for three—no, I'm in error, four—years to bring this project to its fruition.''

They were standing at the entrance of an ancient and royal tomb.

Actually it was the hallway of the Egyptian wing decorated to look like a pharaoh's tomb. The ceiling was painted dark blue. The night skies were etched upon it in gold leaf—stars, constellations, animals and gods and all manner of creatures that inhabited the underworld.

The walls were covered with figures, hieroglyphs and scenes depicting everyday life: farmers tending their fields of grain and flax, flocks of ducks and geese attended by a small boy, vines of lush, dark purple grapes and palm trees hanging heavy with dates, a funeral procession of weeping mourners, warriors engaged in fierce combat against the enemies of the Black Land, the king sitting upon this throne, his queen by his side, followers of the sacred Apis bull cult in the act of worship, priests performing the ceremonies described in the Book of the Dead, including the steps of mummification.

Jonathan paused in front of one segment of the mural and innocently inquired, "What do you suppose this scene represents, *sweetheart?*"

Samantha squinted and took a step closer to the wall, then crimsoned with embarrassment. The scene he was studying showed two figures—an obviously sexually aroused man and a well-endowed nude woman. The female was bending over the male, and there was little doubt as to what was about to take place between them.

"This scene—" Samantha heard her voice crack but she went on in what she hoped was the same no-nonsense tone she used for her lectures at the museum "—represents the divine union of the earth god, Geb, and the sky goddess, Nut. According to ancient Egyptian myth, their union preceded the creation of the world, *darling*."

"Thank you, *sweetheart*," Jonathan murmured politely. Too politely.

"You're welcome, *darling*."

It seemed he wasn't finished. "You know what they say—"

Samantha was half-afraid to ask, but in the end she did. "What?"

"When in doubt, ask the expert."

There was a discreet "ahem" from the waiting footman. They both turned their heads.

"Madam has arranged for you to have the Cleopatra Suite, Professor," he announced, opening the first door on the right side of the hallway. He made a sweeping motion with his arm. "She hopes you will find everything to your satisfaction. If there is anything you need, simply pick up the house telephone and dial the appropriate number. You will find a list on the bedside table."

"Thank you, Martin. You have been most helpful."

"You will be next door in the Ramses Room, Mr. Hazard."

"I'm sure I can find my own way there once I see that the professor is settled in," Jonathan said.

There was no argument from the footman. "Your luggage will be brought up momentarily.

"Thank you again, Martin."

"By the way, we dress for dinner at Fontaine-bleau," he added as the door closed behind him.

The moment they found themselves alone, Samantha turned on her heel, planted her hands on her hips and glowered at Jonathan. She was seething. Her voice rose half an octave. "Gentleman friend?"

His expression bore no trace of an apology. "Hey, it wasn't my idea."

"Maybe not. But why didn't you correct Trout?"

"Why didn't you?"

She was still shaking with anger. "Frankly, I was afraid I'd blow your cover. You should have briefed me."

Jonathan knit his eyebrows. "Briefed you?"

"Told me ahead of time what your cover story was supposed to be."

"I don't have one."

She threw up her hands in a gesture of frustration. "Oh, that's great. That's just great. Some spy you must have been."

"It just so happens that I was a very good spy," he staunchly declared.

"Hmph."

"As it is," Jonathan suggested smoothly, "Trout may have done us a favor."

She was skeptical. "A favor?"

"He's provided us with the perfect cover."

"The perfect cover?" she hooted. "Who in their right mind would believe that you and I are—?"

"Lovers?"

She nodded. "Yes. Lovers."

Jonathan shrugged. "Fortunately, most of the people in this house aren't in their right minds."

Apparently it was contagious.

Samantha was still fuming when she happened to spy a small statue sitting atop a nearby bureau. She picked it up and took a look at it.

"King Khafre," she murmured, studying in detail the copy of the original sculpture. "Khafre was the builder of the second pyramid at Giza and was thought to be the creator of the Great Sphinx."

"It's magnificent," Jonathan said appreciatively.

"Yes." Samantha made a closer examination. "My God, Jonathan," she exclaimed, forgetting for a moment to breathe, forgetting for a moment that she was supposed to be angry with him, "I think it's genuine."

"Genuine?"

She nodded and carefully replaced the ancient stone statue. "This piece probably dates from 2500 B.C. I don't think I've ever seen one of finer quality," she said with reverence. "It belongs in a museum."

"What about the bed?"

Samantha swung around. She took one look at it and groaned. "I only hope I don't get seasick."

He couldn't take his eyes off it.

The bed was the first thing Jonathan saw when

Martin ushered them into the Cleopatra Suite. It was huge, ornate and gaudy. It was shaped like an ancient royal barge, complete with carved rams' heads at the four corners, legs fashioned like the feet of some great mythical beast, gilded headboard and diaphanous silk bedcurtains.

It was the most outrageous bed he had ever laid eyes on. That was his first thought.

How enticing, exciting and downright erotic it would be to lay Samantha down on that bed, slowly strip off her proper little business suit and make wild and wonderful love to her right there and then. That was his second thought.

Bloody hell, Hazard!

It was not his habit to imagine making love to his clients. It was not his habit to mentally undress or fantasize about a woman he had just met, professionally or socially.

He was selective. Very. A smart man had to be, in this day and age.

But a mental picture of Samantha, her lovely long legs wrapped tightly around him, her blond hair falling into disarray around her bare shoulders, her generous breasts with their rosy tips prodding his chest, kept flashing into his mind. It began to do odd things to him.

Sonofa—he was becoming aroused! In fact, he was already partially hard. Another ten seconds and he would embarrass himself if the professor happened to glance down at the front of his jeans.

It was the damnedest thing.

After all, he was a mature man of thirty-six, not some randy sixteen-year-old.

Turning his back on Samantha, he sauntered over to the bedside table and made a production of reading the list of telephone numbers. "Dial 1 for Trout, 2 for Mrs. Danvers, 3 for the kitchens, 4 for the gardener, 5 for the poolside cabana, 6 for the tennis courts, 7 for an outside line." He glanced over his shoulder. "Everything is here but a number for the front desk."

Samantha frowned. "The front desk?"

"Never mind." He was feeling calmer now, more in control of himself. Then he remembered something the footman had said as the door closed. "Dress for dinner? What do you think Martin meant by that?"

"Who doesn't dress for dinner?" she replied.

"The expression usually means formal attire."

That got her attention. "Formal attire?"

"You know, evening dresses for the ladies. Tuxedos for the gentlemen."

Samantha suddenly appeared panic-stricken. "But I didn't bring those kinds of clothes with me."

"Relax. Neither did I." Jonathan rubbed his hand back and forth along his jawline. "Besides, who knows what 'dressing for dinner' really means in this crazy household."

Jonathan had his answer later that afternoon when a polite knock sounded on the door of the Ramses Room.

"Come in," he called out.

The door opened. It was Martin.

"I was instructed to deliver your evening clothes for tonight, Mr. Hazard."

"My evening clothes?"

"Yessir. One tuxedo. One dress shirt. One black tie. One pair of dress socks and shoes." Martin carefully laid out each item on the bed. "Mr. Trout judged you to be a forty-two-long jacket, a thirty-four-inch waist, a size sixteen shirt and an eleven shoe."

He was impressed. Damned impressed. "That's amazing. How does Trout do it?"

"I don't know, sir. But he hasn't been wrong once in all the years I've been at Fontainebleau."

Jonathan's interest was piqued. "What was delivered next door to Professor Wainwright?"

"A gown in emerald green silk. Size eight." With that, Martin made his exit.

As Jonathan dressed for dinner, he recalled a moment yesterday afternoon at the Kemet Museum. He had tried to picture Samantha Wainwright with her hair undone wearing an emerald green dress that matched the color of her eyes.

It seemed he wouldn't have to rely on his imagination much longer.

Five

"So much for your disguise," Samantha informed him when she saw Jonathan that evening.

He was Bond. James Bond. 007. Licensed to kill. Lady-killer. Suave. Debonair. Born to wear a tuxedo. Tall, dark and handsome. And utterly irresistible to women.

"Whatever you do," she warned, "don't order a martini shaken, not stirred. It would be a dead give-away."

Jonathan didn't say a word. He just stood there in the doorway of the Cleopatra Suite and stared at her.

Samantha could feel the heat rising in her cheeks. "Is something wrong?"

He shook his head.

"I feel a little silly," she admitted, reminding herself *not* to wipe her palms on the flowing green silk dress that seemed to naturally cling to her body in all the wrong places.

Perhaps she should have pulled her hair back in its usual bun.

Perhaps she should have worn her glasses, even if she didn't need them all the time.

Perhaps she shouldn't have applied the touch of blush to her cheeks or the lipstick to her mouth.

Perhaps she should have left well enough alone.

Jonathan finally spoke. His voice sounded slightly husky to her. "I've waited a lifetime to see you in something emerald green and clinging."

"A lifetime?" Samantha laughed self-consciously. "We've only known each other since yesterday afternoon."

His dark eyebrows drew together in a studied frown. "Haven't you heard the expression 'what a difference a day makes?' "

He took a purposeful step toward her, and just for a moment—a tense, heart-stopping, anticipatory moment—Samantha thought he was going to kiss her.

Then a strange sound, faintly reminiscent of a huge brass Tibetan gong, rang out from somewhere within the vast recesses of the castle.

"Saved by the gong," Jonathan muttered with a rueful smile.

Samantha glanced down at the watch on her wrist. She noticed her hands were trembling. Damn, she just wasn't any good with men. She never had been. She never would be. "Eight o'clock on the dot," she said nervously. "I assume we're being summoned to dinner."

Jonathan graciously offered her his arm. "First, cocktails are served in the library. At least according to Martin."

"Martin should know."

She placed her hand on the sleeve of Jonathan's elegant evening jacket, hoping he wouldn't notice how skittish she was feeling, how cool to the touch her fingertips suddenly were. They made their way through the pharaoh's tomb, along the rows of cabinets containing the valuable Meissen porcelain and down the sweeping staircase.

The library was empty. Evidently they were the first to arrive. Within a minute or two, however, Trout appeared with a drinks tray.

"Would you care for a dry sherry, Professor?"

"Thank you, Trout."

"Mr. Hazard?"

"Chivas Regal. Soda. No ice."

"Of course, sir," the butler said approvingly.

"And Trout—"

"Yes, Mr. Hazard?"

"Thank you for sending up the appropriate evening clothes for Professor Wainwright and myself."

"You are most welcome, sir."

"Maybe one day you'll tell me your secret."

Frowning, Trout regarded the other man. "My secret, sir?"

"How you determine the correct sizes...right down to the shoes."

The butler's forehead smoothed out. "Perhaps one day I will, Mr. Hazard."

The library door opened and a woman entered. She was closer to sixty than fifty, with steel gray eyes, and equally steel gray hair pulled back into a tight, unflattering knot at the back of her head. Her chin was pointed. Her nose was long and thin and pinched.

So was her face.

She was dressed in a plain gray dress and wore not a speck of makeup. There was no nonsense about her. Her movements were spare, quick, efficient. She didn't look to her right or left, but focused straight ahead. She didn't acknowledge their presence in the room, and she certainly did not smile. She simply went about the business of arranging the platters of hot and cold hors d'oeuvres.

Mrs. Danvers.

With a pang, Samantha realized that in another thirty years, *she* could be this woman. She could be living life without joy, without love, without passion. If she wasn't careful, she could end up a bitter, sour, dried-up, shriveled-up old maid.

She took a tentative step toward the housekeeper and said in a cordial tone, "You must be Mrs. Danvers. I'm Samantha Wainwright, and this is Jonathan Hazard."

The woman glanced up and gave each of them a brusque nod. "Professor. Mr. Hazard." Her task completed, she turned and exited the room.

"Not exactly the friendly type, is she?" Jonathan observed, shaking his head.

Samantha stared down into her glass of dry sherry. "No, she isn't."

"Of course, you did warn me."

She looked up. "*I* warned you?"

He lowered his voice and said conspiratorially, "About Mrs. Danvers."

Samantha hastened to explain. "*That* Mrs. Danvers was a fictional character in a book published more than fifty years ago."

Jonathan took a sip of his Scotch and soda. "She was the villainess of the story, right?"

"She was."

"A murderess who went out in a blaze of glory."

Samantha tried not to groan. "That was a terrible pun."

A faint look of amusement crossed Jonathan's handsome face. "Puns usually are terrible, by definition."

She took in a deep breath and slowly let it out again. "Where do you suppose everyone else is?"

As if on cue, a man sauntered into the room. He was short and slightly rotund. His hair was dark—what there was of it—and his complexion was deeply tanned. He had full lips, full cheeks and several chins. There was an unlit cigar clenched between his front teeth and a ring on his pinkie sporting a diamond the size of a bird's egg.

He plucked the cigar from his mouth and extended his hand first to Samantha and then to Jonathan. His grip was surprisingly soft. "Howdy, folks. I'm Crispy Green. I heard we had company. Sure is nice to see a fresh face around here, and such a pretty one, too." He winked at Samantha.

She resisted the urge to wipe off her hand on her cocktail napkin. "How do you do, Mr. Green. I'm Samantha Wainwright, and this is Jonathan Hazard."

He clasped her by the elbow and, drawing her aside for a moment, inquired in a theatrical whisper, "Tell me, what's a nice girl like you doing in a place like this?"

Samantha gritted her teeth and counted to ten. "I am an Egyptologist, Mr. Green."

"An Egyptologist," he repeated, shaking his balding head in disbelief. "You mean King Tut and all that stuff?"

She nodded. "King Tut and all that stuff." Samantha reminded herself that she had dealt with ignorance before.

Crispy Green began to snort. "I've got a great joke for you, honey."

Samantha grimaced.

The man's belly began to shake beneath his white dress shirt and plaid cummerbund. "Do you know what one Egyptologist said to the other?"

"I'm afraid not."

Crispy Green slapped his thigh. "How's your mummy?" He put his head back and guffawed. "Get it? Mommy. Mummy. How's your mummy?"

Samantha hid behind the very small glass of sherry she held in her hand.

The newcomer wiped the tears from his eyes, stuck the unlit cigar back in his mouth and rolled it around between his lips. "What do you do, Mr. Hazard?"

"I—"

He didn't wait for an answer. "I'm in business myself. Big business. I wheel and I deal. As a matter of fact, I've recently pulled off a couple of big ones for the prince. Hell, he wouldn't take a leak without my say-so. I've done some major deals in my time. I swim with the sharks. But you wouldn't know about that, would you, boy?"

Samantha sucked in her breath. Jonathan's eyes narrowed. His lips went thin. A muscle in his jaw began to twitch. He seemed to grow taller and his shoulders broader.

Crispy Green was treading on thin ice. She wondered if he had any idea how thin. The buffoon imagined himself to be a man, and a dangerous one at that. It was ludicrous. Laughable. He wasn't dangerous.

Jonathan was dangerous.

It was crystal clear to her. Why couldn't Crispy Green see it?

Jonathan stepped directly in front of the offensive little toad and stared down at him. In a deceptively mild tone she heard him say, "I believe you asked me a minute ago what I do, Mr. Green."

Beads of perspiration suddenly formed along the other man's forehead and upper lip. "I...believe I did."

"I don't swim with the sharks." He deliberately dropped his voice. "I *am* one of the sharks."

Crispy Green paled. "I need a drink, Trout."

"Of course, Mr. Green."

"My usual."

The butler arched a quizzical eyebrow and managed to add insult to injury. "Your usual, sir?"

"Yes, dammit, my usual. I'll have a whiskey. In fact, make it a double." The semipermanent houseguest dug around in the pocket of his dress trousers and extracted a handkerchief. He mopped the sweat from his face. "Warm evening, isn't it, folks?" He took a gulp of his drink. "I see Carlotta and the prince aren't down yet."

It was Trout who replied. "They should be momentarily."

Crispy chewed on the end of his stogie. "No smoking allowed in the house, you know," he remarked to no one in particular. "Have you met our host and hostess?"

"No, I haven't," Samantha confessed.

"You're in for a treat."

A *surprise* was more like it.

For the third time that evening, the library door opened. In swept a small woman in floor-length pink chiffon. Her throat and bosom were dripping with pink pearls. A pink hat of fine pink feathers, fashioned in the shape of a pink swan, was perched on her pink hair. A small pink dog was tucked under her arm.

Crispy Green advanced toward the creature in pink, made a production of kissing her hand, and exclaimed in a raspy voice that sounded like he had smoked one too many Havanas, "Carlotta, you look ravishing this evening."

"Thank you, my dear Crispy."

The lady glanced at her butler. "Pink champagne, I think, Trout."

"Yes, Madam."

"These must be our guests," she surmised, bearing down upon Samantha and Jonathan. "You are Professor Samantha Wainwright. I am Carlotta McDonnell."

"It's a pleasure meeting you, Mrs. McDonnell. Thank you for making me feel welcome."

The woman's eyes were shrewd. She was not, perhaps, quite the brainless creature in pink chiffon that she presented herself to be. "You must be terribly bright, my dear. Egyptology. I understand that you will know all about the 'things' that Archie collected."

"I hope so. I'm eager to begin."

"And you will begin first thing in the morning, if you wish. But tonight we will share a lovely little dinner together." She took a sip of her pink champagne. "You are a very tall, Professor."

"Five feet eight inches, I'm afraid."

"You are also very beautiful."

Samantha blushed. "Thank you, Mrs. McDonnell."

"Modest, too. I like that. I like you. You may call me Carlotta, and I will call you Samantha."

"If you wish."

Their hostess put her head back even farther and gazed up at Jonathan. "What a lot of very tall people there seem to be about these days." She sniffed. "You must be—"

"Jonathan Hazard."

"The boyfriend?"

"Yes."

She glanced at Samantha. "You must have your hands full with this one."

Jonathan grinned. "She does, indeed."

Carlotta returned to him. "Are you a comedian of some sort, Mr. Hazard?"

"No, I am not, Mrs. McDonnell."

"An actor?"

He shook his head. "I'm not an actor, either."

"What are you, then?"

"Frankly, I have been many things," he told her, "including a geologist."

Despite the difference in their heights, Samantha watched as Carlotta McDonnell looked Jonathan square in the eyes. "You don't seem to be like the kind of man who spends his time examining rocks."

"My specialty was petroleum."

"Ah—oil." The woman studied him over the rim of her crystal champagne glass. "You are a bit too handsome for your own good, but you may call me Carlotta. I like handsome men."

"I like women who wear pink well."

That made her laugh. "You're charming, too. You'll have to keep your eye on him, Samantha."

"Every second," she agreed.

Trout cleared his throat and announced with a flourish, "Prince Henri."

Samantha half expected to hear a drumroll or, at the very least, the clarion call of a trumpet. What in the world did you say to a man who had crowned himself a prince, anyway?

Henry McDonnell—dress uniform perfectly pressed, ribbons all aflutter and medals polished—acknowledged his wife first. *"Bonsoir, chère."*

"Henry, my dear."

Next, he bestowed his attention on Crispy Green. "Monsieur Green."

The wheeler-dealer clicked his heels together and bowed from his ample waist. "Prince Henri."

"And these must be our newly arrived guests."

"May I have the pleasure of introducing Professor Samantha Wainwright, a world-renowned Egyptologist, and Mister Jonathan Hazard."

"Charmant! Très charmant!" the prince exclaimed as he greeted Samantha.

Jonathan was right about one thing. The man's accent was an atrocity. Still, she managed a respectable curtsy. "It is an honor to meet you, Prince Henri."

Henry McDonnell beamed. Apparently, she had said and done the right thing.

Then he turned to Jonathan. "Monsieur Gizzard."

"Mister Hazard, my dear," Carlotta gently corrected her husband.

"Monsieur."

"Sir."

Trout appeared with a glass of French wine. "Your Chablis, Prince Henri."

"*Merci,* Trout." Then he made a sweeping gesture that seemed to encompass the entire castle as well as the library. "How do you like Fontainebleau?"

"It is an incredible house," Samantha declared.

The prince frowned. "House?"

She quickly corrected herself. "It is an incredible castle."

"*Mais oui!* My great-uncle was particularly taken with the original *château* in France, so he had his own built. He was that kind of man. *Formidable!*"

"Archie was remarkable, all right," said Carlotta.

"Remarkable," echoed Crispy Green.

"We must give you the grand tour while you are with us," the prince suggested.

"We'll both look forward to that." She smiled at Jonathan. "Won't we, *darling?*"

There was a flash of perfectly straight white teeth. "Of course, *sweetheart.*"

Henry McDonnell must have given a signal. Trout immediately appeared at his side, dispensed with the prince's half-empty glass of Chablis and announced, "Dinner is served."

The prince extended his arm to Samantha. Jonathan graciously escorted Carlotta, but not before she handed over the small bundle of pink fur to Trout. "Henry simply will not allow dogs in the dining room."

"Do you like dogs, Mr. Hazard?" their hostess inquired once they were settled at the mahogany dining-room table that could have easily seated twenty.

"Dogs are often a man's or a woman's best friend," Samantha heard him answer discreetly.

"Do you have any pets?"

"It is difficult for someone who travels as much as I do," he said.

Difficult, but certainly not impossible, thought Samantha.

Jonathan cleverly worked the conversation back to Carlotta. "You must be very fond of dogs."

She popped a small poached sea scallop topped with beluga and golden caviar into her mouth, delicately chewed for a moment and then swallowed before she replied. "Especially my Pekingese. I have fourteen, you know."

"Really."

"All of them are absolute dears."

Henry McDonnell had apparently heard enough about his wife's precious dogs. He turned to Samantha. "Have you been to Paris, Professor?"

"Regrettably, no."

"You must go one day. It is the most *magnifique* city in the entire world."

"And the most romantic," interjected Carlotta. She looked meaningfully from Jonathan to Samantha. "How long have you two known each other?"

Samantha choked on a bite of beluga. "Oh, a long time," she finally managed.

Jonathan's eyes flickered almost humorously. "But it seems like we met just yesterday, doesn't it?"

She shot daggers at him. "Yes. It does."

Between spoonfuls of quail consommé, garnished with stuffed morels, their hostess seemed intent on playing matchmaker. "Have you set a date?"

Samantha looked at the petite woman, uncomprehending. "A date?"

"A wedding date?"

Samantha was speechless.

"My, my." Carlotta clicked her tongue disapprovingly, "You young people are always so busy with your careers. You must have a large church wedding with all the trimmings," she admonished them, "and a grand reception and a glorious honeymoon. After all, you only get married once—with any luck, of course."

"When I get married, it will be forever," Jonathan stated emphatically.

Carlotta McDonnell was a first-class snoop. "How many children do you want?"

Samantha put her soup spoon down. "I haven't really thought about children."

Simultaneously Jonathan answered, "Two—a boy and a girl."

They were digging themselves deeper and deeper into a hole, Samantha realized. And they might never manage to get out again. At least not while they were in residence at Fontainebleau.

How could she keep up the pretense of being in love with Jonathan Hazard for the next three weeks when all she really wanted to do was choke the man?

"You never told us," promoted Carlotta. "How did you two meet?"

Jonathan seemed perfectly willing to answer the question for both of them. "I've spent quite a lot of time in the Middle East as a petroleum expert and adviser to various companies. Samantha has been traveling to Egypt with her father for... how many years, sweetheart?"

He was the expert. Let him figure it out. "Since I was eleven years old," she said.

Jonathan gave a private laugh. "We like to think it was ancient Egypt that brought us together."

Carlotta sighed, "How romantic," and rested her little pink hand on her little pink chin.

For the first time in her life, Samantha Wainwright wished her legs were even longer. She would enjoy nothing more at that moment than kicking Jonathan Hazard under the table. The man was placing her in an untenable position.

Why?

Why was he trying to drive her nuts?

Something about her drove him nuts!

From the first instant he had walked into her office at the Kemet Museum, she had gotten under his skin and irritated the hell out of him. It was that cool, icy exterior she presented to the world, when he knew damn well she was molten lava on the inside, just waiting to erupt.

Things had come to a head when he'd stood in the doorway of her suite tonight and watched as a vision in emerald green walked toward him. Jonathan had wanted to take her in his arms and kiss her until she couldn't see, couldn't breathe, couldn't stand on her own two feet. Hell, until she couldn't even sit up straight.

He wanted to kiss Samantha Wainwright silly.

He wanted to kiss her until she could think, smell, feel, taste, imagine only him.

He wanted to kiss her until she forgot every other man and every other kiss in her life.

Realization dawned. He was losing it. He'd better get a grip on himself or this would end up being the longest evening of his entire life. And he'd endured some pretty long evenings.

Jonathan recalled one in particular.

Bangkok, or *Krung Thep*, "City of Angels" as the Thais called it. Ninteen eighty-seven. His old nemesis had finally caught up with him in a back alley. He'd been fished out of the *khlongs* the next morning by a friendly local, and spent a month in the hospital recovering. Yet there hadn't been a single visible mark on his body.

He would not let Samantha Wainwright get to him like that. He would not allow her to tear him to pieces and leave him for dead.

Enough was enough.

There was still the rest of dinner to be endured. Not to mention cigars and brandy afterward, perhaps even a game of billiards with the gentlemen. Then the obligatory cup of coffee with the ladies. It was going to be hours, not minutes, until he could escort Samantha back to the Cleopatra Suite.

And then what?

He could hardly invite himself in and stay for the night. She wasn't that kind of woman. Hell, he didn't even know what kind of woman she was when it came to men.

Yes, he did.

She was uncomfortable with men, uncomfortable with sex, uncomfortable with her own physical attractiveness. She was a woman who had spent her life being smart, and yet she was still dumb. She was intelligent, rather sweet and naive, sexually inexperienced, and wholly infuriating.

She was one in a million and—as he had instinctively known from the beginning—Samantha Wainwright was going to be a royal pain in the butt!

God knows how he made it through dinner, but he did: making urbane small talk, laughing in all the right places, telling stories that had entertained so many others before, asking Carlotta and the prince the kind of questions that they obviously enjoyed answering. He even managed to draw information out of Crispy Green.

Jonathan declined the cigar offered but sipped half a brandy while he played billiards with the prince, allowing the other man to just beat him on the second and third games.

It was eleven before the gentlemen rejoined the ladies for coffee and a sweet. It was closer to midnight before Jonathan found himself alone with Samantha. They were strolling toward the Egyptian wing of the great house.

"This has been quite an evening," he said.

She sighed. "Now I know how Alice felt."

"Alice?"

"Alice in Wonderland when she fell down the rabbit hole and found herself in a strange, irrational world filled with strange, irrational people."

"We even have a Mad Hatter."

"Carlotta is actually very kind."

"Snoopy."

"That, too," she agreed, shivering. There was a definite chill in the passageway. "The prince seems harmless enough. But you're right about his French accent. It's awful. Poor man."

Jonathan shrugged off his dress jacket and slipped it around Samantha's shoulders. "I don't know what I would be like if I'd grown up in the shadow of Archibald McDonnell and his billions and billions of dollars."

"I think you would be the same."

"Thank you." He frowned. "I think."

Samantha picked up her skirts as they climbed the flight of stairs. "You were very good with them."

"I like Carlotta and the prince."

She made an expressive face. "I don't like Crispy Green."

"The man is a—" Jonathan bit off the word on the tip of his tongue.

"Buffoon?"

He laughed out of the side of his mouth. "Right."

Samantha gently placed her hand on his shirtsleeve. "You showed great restraint when he called you 'boy.'"

"I wanted to knock his lousy teeth in."

"I know. But you didn't."

"No. I didn't."

"Well, here we are," she said, pausing in front of the Cleopatra Suite. She smiled up at him. "Thank you for walking me home."

Jonathan rested his arm against the door on one side of her head. "You are stunning in that green dress."

"Thank you."

"It clings in all the right places."

He saw her swallow nervously. "Does it?"

"There is one thing I've been wanting to do all evening—"

Instantly, a wary expression sprang into her emerald green eyes. "What is that?"

Jonathan reached out and gently grasped a handful of hair. He let a few silky strands fall through his fingers like a cloud of gold dust. "It's beautiful," he murmured. "You should wear it down more often."

"It . . . uh . . . gets in my way."

"Somehow I don't think that's the only reason," he said to her.

"It's more businesslike to wear it up."

"I suppose so." He added, "You look about twenty years old with it tumbling down around your shoulders."

"That's another reason I wear it up."

Jonathan leaned toward Samantha and buried his face in her hair, taking a deep breath. "It feels so good. It smells so good."

"Jonathan—"

"Hmm." He nuzzled her neck.

"What are you doing?"

"What do you think I'm doing?"

She sounded out of breath. "I—I don't know."

"What do you think I'm *going* to do?"

"I don't know."

"What do you *want* me to do?"

Samantha pressed her hands against his chest and put an inch or two between them. "What do I want you to do?" she repeated.

Jonathan nodded.

She let out a long sigh, gazed up into his eyes and said, "I want you to kiss me."

And so he did.

Six

"**On** second thought, I don't think this is a good idea." Samantha panicked at the last moment.

"Neither do I," Jonathan agreed.

Her heart was pounding in her ears. "You don't?"

"No. I don't."

Jonathan's face was so close to hers that she could see each individual eyelash, the dark stubble of his beard, the slight flare of his nostrils, the small indentation above his upper lip, the shape of his mouth.

He had a beautiful mouth.

His breath was warm and fragrant on her skin. He smelled slightly of coffee and expensive brandy. It wasn't unpleasant. In fact, it was just the opposite. It was enticing. Masculine. Heady.

"Maybe we should talk about it." Samantha struggled to keep her voice even.

"That sounds like something a woman would suggest at a time like this," Jonathan said with a laugh. His laugh made her spine tingle.

She pushed back her hair. "I don't kiss strangers."

"Neither do I."

He was staring at her mouth. It made it difficult for her to concentrate on what she had to say. "Ours is strictly a professional relationship."

"Never mix business and pleasure."

"I feel exactly the same way."

"Then we see eye to eye on the subject."

"Besides—" Samantha paused significantly "—I'm just not any good at this kind of thing."

Jonathan blinked. "What kind of thing?"

She swallowed hard. "Men."

"Men?"

Her heart sank. "Kissing."

He waited.

"Making out."

He stood there.

She winced. "Sexual desire. Physical passion. Whatever it is that's supposed to happen between a man and a woman." Tears stung her eyes. "Haven't you heard, Mr. Hazard. I'm as cold as Arctic ice."

"Bull."

Her breath caught audibly. "I—I beg your pardon."

"There's nothing wrong with you," he stated.

How would he know? He was no expert on the subject of her sex life . . . or the absence thereof. The man had never even kissed her, for crying out loud.

"As a matter of fact," Jonathan declared, "You are the most passionate woman I have ever met."

"I am?"

"You are."

Samantha tilted her head to one side and looked at him askance. "Is this the nineties version of the eighties seduction scene?"

"Absolutely not."

"Scout's honor?"

"Scout's honor." Then Jonathan took her face in his hands. "There is a big difference, Samantha, between inexperience and inability."

She summoned her courage. "Frankly, I don't have much in the way of experience."

"Good."

"Good?"

He seemed relieved, even pleased. "You can't be too careful in this day and age."

"Careful?"

He spelled it out for her. "Personal hygiene. Cleanliness. Safe sex. Absence of communicable diseases."

"And you?"

"I can guarantee you a clean bill of health." Suddenly, his voice grew softer; he was almost caressing her with his words. "I want to kiss you, Samantha."

Her heart began to slam against her ribs. "Do you want to kiss me or the creature in the emerald green dress?"

"You are the creature in the emerald green dress."

Her voice caught. "It's not really me."

"Of course it is."

She shook her head. "It's the dress."

"It isn't."

"It is."

A dangerous glint appeared in Jonathan's eyes. "Then take the dress off and you'll know for sure."

Samantha couldn't help herself. She laughed out loud. "That was very clever."

He grinned devilishly. "I thought so."

She stopped laughing. "I'm afraid."

"I know."

"I'm a little nervous."

"So am I."

"My hands are cold."

"Then be careful where you put them." Apparently, Jonathan ran out of patience at that point. He swooped down and took her mouth, muttering, "To hell with it. You can put your hands anywhere you want."

Jonathan wanted to be more specific. He wanted desperately to tell Samantha, encourage Samantha, show Samantha, where he'd like her to put her hands.

There were parts of him that were itching to be scratched, needing to be touched, begging to be caressed. She could start at the top and work her way down. She could begin at the bottom and work her way up. She could go straight to the middle and skip the rest.

Just the thought of her long, cool, elegant fingers on his flesh was nearly enough to drive Jonathan over the edge.

Cold? Once they got going, neither one of them would be cold for long. That was a promise.

Whoa! He was getting way ahead of the game, Jonathan cautioned himself.

This was their first kiss. It wouldn't be their last if he had anything to say or do about it, but he knew Samantha was nervous, skittish. He had to take it slow and easy, or he'd scare her off.

Scaring her off was the last thing he was interested in doing.

Jonathan took a tentative taste of her lips. They were soft, warm, surprisingly willing. Her mouth was sweeter than wine and far more intoxicating. She went straight to his head. And to a few other places . . .

His hands found the front of his tuxedo jacket, which was still draped around her. He grasped the lapels in his fists and urged her toward him. Her body slammed up against his. He could feel her from shoulder to knee.

Her breasts were round, firm, generous. Her nipples curled into tight little excited buds that poked him in the chest. For a moment, he imagined what those rosy tips would look like, feel like, taste like.

Jonathan groaned. ''Samantha—'' He wasn't even sure he had spoken her name aloud until she responded.

''What is it?'' she mumbled against his mouth.

''You,'' was all he could manage.

His hands encircled her waist. She was sleek, slim, slender. Her stomach was flat. Her thighs were strong and slightly muscular, just right for a man to settle himself between while he went about discovering other muscles, secret muscles, wonderfully feminine muscles.

The woman was getting to him. Jonathan could detect the changes in his own body—the increased heart rate, the rapid breathing, the blood pounding in his temples, the tensed muscles in his arms and legs, the tightening of his groin, the thickening of his manhood.

He urged Samantha's lips apart, and dipped and delved into her mouth, engaging her in an erotic duel. It was thrust and parry; it was the clash of teeth and tongues and sensitized skin. She was all sweetness and light one instant, intense, smoldering sensuality the next.

His fingertips traced a path from her waist to her rib cage, from her rib cage to her breasts. She seemed to swell to fill his hands. Through the silky material of the emerald green dress, her nipples teased and tantalized him.

Then he slipped his hands around to her back, cupped her derriere in his palms and pressed her against him. There wasn't a shadow of a doubt now.

Samantha would know exactly what effect she had on him. He was hard as nails and he was up-front about the fact.

"Ohmigod, Jonathan." She brought her head up, gasping for air. "What if someone should see us?"

"Who?"

She made a frantic gesture. "Somebody. Anybody. The McDonnells. The servants."

"The dogs?"

She gave him one of those looks.

"Don't worry, honey. There's no one here but the two of us, and the night does not have eyes," he assured her.

Her eyes were troubled. "What about security? Concealed microphones? Hidden video cameras?"

"I've already made a thorough check of the hallway and both of our bedrooms."

That created a raised eyebrow or two.

"Old habits die hard," Jonathan explained. "Anyway, there's nothing. Negative. *Nada.*"

Samantha concentrated on her hands. "Are you certain?"

"Dead certain."

She raised her head suddenly and there was alarm on her face as she stared up into his. "This is too much, too soon, too fast for me, Jonathan."

He leaned forward and rested his forehead against hers. "I won't say that I'm sorry because I'd be lying. But I honestly didn't mean for it to go this far."

"Neither did I."

"Maybe now you'll believe me, though."

Her eyes were still clouded with passion. "Believe you?"

"When I tell you that there's nothing wrong with you, that you aren't as cold as Arctic ice, that you are the most passionate woman I have ever met."

She chewed on her lower lip. "I don't understand it. I was never like this before."

He sighed and suggested, "Maybe it was the right time and the right place this time."

A small line of concentration formed between her eyes. "Do you really believe that?"

He glanced up at the colorful, exotic and sometimes erotic paintings on the walls surrounding them. "Maybe it was the artwork that put us in the proper frame of mind."

Samantha immediately stepped back and began to tap her foot rhythmically on the hardwood floor. "I see. Then you took your inspiration from the earth god, Geb, and the sky goddess, Nut, and their 'symbolic' union."

Too late.

It was too bloody late by the time Jonathan realized he had made a grave strategical error.

"You know what they say, don't you, Mr. Hazard?"

He didn't want to ask. "What?"

"One man's treasure is another man's trash."

"Huh?"

"Let me paraphrase that for you—one man's art is another man's dirty pictures."

"Now, Sam, honey—"

"Do not call me Sam and do not call me honey. And the next time you get turned on by some erotic depiction of the sexual act, find someone else to play out your little games with."

"I wasn't playing little games."

She arched a blond eyebrow. "*Big* games, then?"

"I wasn't playing any kind of game," he informed her.

"What do you call it, then?" she sniffed.

The woman was deliberately being obtuse. She was damned infuriating, too! "I call it kissing that got a bit out of hand."

"A bit out of hand?"

"Okay, a lot out of hand. We got excited. We were sexually aroused. We kissed. We touched. We caressed in a very intimate manner. It undoubtedly crossed our minds that we might like to make love to each other."

"Speak for yourself," Samantha snapped.

"I was." A bucket of ice water couldn't have put out the fire of his desire any faster or more completely. "But don't kid yourself, lady. You enjoyed it as much as I did. You were aroused, too. You were just as hot and bothered as I was. Hell, you were burning up in my hands."

"Thank you, Mr. Hazard," she stated with stiff formality as she tore off his jacket and threw it at him. "This has been—shall we say—a truly edifying experience."

His mouth twisted into a suggestive smile. "Any time, Professor."

The last thing Jonathan Hazard saw and heard was the door of Samantha Wainwright's bedroom slamming shut in his face.

Seven

———

"**O**n second thought, I don't think this is a good idea," the woman said, lowering her voice to a mere whisper.

"Neither do I," the man agreed.

"My heart's pounding so fast it feels like it's going to burst in my chest," she confessed, pressing her hand dramatically to her bosom.

"Mine, too," he grumbled.

"I don't like it."

"I don't, either."

"Perhaps we ought to tell Trout."

"Tell Trout!"

"Shhhh!" she hissed. "Keep your voice down. Do you want to wake the dead?"

He glanced nervously from side to side, then stated emphatically, "We can't tell Trout."

She sighed. "You're right."

"Of course, I'm right."

"Then maybe we can figure out another plan of action," she suggested after a moment.

He snickered softly in the dark. "Like what?"

"I don't know." She was struggling to keep her voice even. "But this one scares me. It doesn't feel right. In fact, it feels *wrong*."

"That sounds like some damned-fool thing a woman would think of at a time like this," her companion complained.

She was tempted to box his ears for his insolence. "It's called a woman's intuition and it has saved your sorry neck more than once."

He mumbled something unintelligible.

She pushed back her hair. That's when she noticed her hands were trembling. She folded them in her lap, tightly intertwined her fingers and willed herself to remain calm. "We wouldn't be in this mess if it weren't for you."

"It's not my fault," the man whined. "He's got me by the—"

"I'll have none of your vulgarities," she snapped. "The truth is he's got you exactly where he wants you."

The man's face paled in the moonlight that streamed in through the window. "I don't see any way out except to do what he tells me to."

She pursed her lips and suggested thoughtfully, "That is because you have no imagination."

"And no brains," he grumbled.

He'd said it, not her.

"As you have seen fit to tell me again and again," he added.

She cautioned herself to patience. She still needed him—at least for a while longer. "Stop your whining, we have work to do."

"What work?"

"The big storeroom."

"The big storeroom?"

"In the Egyptian wing."

"What about it?"

"It's time we took a look."

"Why?"

"Because sooner or later our newly arrived guests will start poking around in there, and the professor is no fool." A frown creased her forehead. "Neither is the man with her who says he's her boyfriend."

"Isn't he?"

She tapped a fingernail against her bottom lip. "I don't know. But I'd be willing to bet that there is more to Mr. Hazard than meets the eye." She gave herself a good shake. "Everybody should be asleep by now. We don't have any time to waste. I'll carry the flashlight. You bring the satchel."

"What do we need a satchel for?"

"In case we find anything of value." She glanced back over her shoulder at him. "Do try to be quiet. No talking out loud. And don't shuffle your feet when you walk."

He silently tiptoed along behind her for several minutes. Then he came up and whispered in her ear, "But why the old storeroom? It's filled with nothing but junk."

"We don't know that for certain." She slipped on a pair of gloves as they went. There was no sense in leaving incriminating fingerprints. "What we do know is that Archie kept very accurate records of the valuables in the rest of the house. If we tried to sell any of those, it would be too obvious."

"We'd get caught."

"*You* would get caught."

The man gulped. "I could go to jail."

"Only if you were lucky enough to escape *him,*" she said brutally.

"Do you really think he would—?"

She inhaled a deep, trembling breath. "Yes, unfortunately, I do."

She could smell his fear.

"He would kill me for a few lousy thousand—?"

"Or he'd have you killed."

There was something she wasn't telling him, of course. He wasn't the only one in trouble. She was, too. Their nemesis was a very clever man. He'd made sure he had something incriminating on both of them.

Insurance, he had called it, laughing cruelly in her face.

She paused for a moment and looked at the man beside her matter-of-factly. If only one of them could survive . . . she intended to make sure it was her.

Eight

Combat pay.

It was no less than he deserved, Jonathan told himself as he recalled the "shots" Samantha had taken at him in the past week, since *that* night, their first night at Fontainebleau, the night he had kissed her in the hallway outside the Cleopatra Suite.

The lady was a deadly shot.

Cheap shots.

Potshots.

With both barrels.

Below the belt.

Right between the eyes.

Bull's-eye.

Yup, Samantha Wainwright held a grudge real well. She had her mind made up; there was no sense in confusing her with the facts. She was convinced that any woman would have served his purposes, that she just happened to be handy—no pun intended—when he had become sexually aroused by the wallpaper.

Jonathan punched at the bed pillows propped up behind his head. The wallpaper? If it weren't so damned asinine, it would be funny.

It all went to show how naive Samantha really was. And how vulnerable. She had no confidence—zilch— in her own attractiveness. Which was a shame because the lady was a knockout. At least she had the potential to be a knockout once she let her hair down, literally and figuratively.

She sure knew how to give a cold shoulder. Hers had become downright frigid. She was excruciatingly polite to him, of course. It drove him nuts. *She* drove him nuts.

Truce.

It was time they declared a truce, Jonathan decided as he lay staring at the ceiling in the Ramses Room, counting the elegant kohl-eyed figures in ancient Egyptian garments, the row upon row of lettered hieroglyphs, and what appeared to be ducks and falcons, cows and cats lined up for some purpose he failed to comprehend.

If Samantha were stretched out beside him, she could undoubtedly explain the entire story on the ceiling, telling him what each figure and letter represented.

Of course, if Samantha were stretched out beside him on the bed, they would have far better things to do than stare at the ceiling. . . .

Truce.

This morning he was determined to break through the seemingly insurmountable barrier she had erected between them, and see if he could work his way back to square one.

Jonathan sighed and threw off the covers. He hadn't been able to keep his hands off her that night. It had been stupid. *He* had been stupid. He should have known better than to rush a woman like Samantha. But his desire for her had taken over and he had lost control. He had behaved like a jackass.

Speaking of which, there was a rather nicely done donkey on one section of the ceiling that he'd missed before. Maybe there was a message in that for him.

A man was damned if he did, and damned if he didn't.

With that final thought on the subject of women, Jonathan rolled out of bed and headed for the shower.

This morning they were inspecting some kind of storeroom. Samantha had informed him that she had completed her preliminary examination of the Egyptian wing, as far as the first-rate antiquities were concerned.

The task had been made infinitely easier by the fact that Archibald McDonnell had left behind a detailed list of the artifacts he had acquired, how much he had paid for each one, where and when they were purchased, and any available historical background information.

The man had been a stickler for detail. Little wonder he had accumulated so much wealth in his long and illustrious business career.

Twenty minutes later—showered, shaved, dressed in his usual blue jeans, work shirt and sneakers, and ready to face the day—Jonathan stepped from his bedroom the moment he heard Samantha's door open.

She was dressed in an unflattering green suit—except for the color, it was identical to every other suit she owned—and a pair of matching unflattering green pumps. Her hair was pulled straight back. Her tortoiseshell glasses were neatly in place. There was a notebook tucked under her arm and a pen clasped in her hand. She was wearing a loose smock that hit her midthigh; it was faintly reminiscent of a lab coat.

"Good morning, Professor." Jonathan greeted her with unrelenting cheerfulness.

She gave a decisive nod of her head. "Good morning, Mr. Hazard."

"How are you this morning?"

"I'm fine."

"Did you sleep well?"

"Certainly."

"Did you enjoy breakfast?" Trays were delivered to their respective rooms by the kitchen staff.

"Of course I enjoyed breakfast," she said, and took off down the hall.

He fell into step beside her. "I thought the sticky buns were particularly delicious, didn't you?"

"I wouldn't know. I don't eat sticky buns, or any kind of pastries, for that matter."

Jonathan made a sympathetic clicking sound with his tongue. "That's a shame. Life is short, and you're missing the sweetest parts."

They both knew he wasn't talking about breakfast rolls.

Samantha glanced at her wristwatch, muttered, "It's nearly eight o'clock and time to get to work," put her head down and barreled forward.

Jonathan reached out and grabbed her gently but firmly by the elbow. "Samantha..."

She stopped. Her head came up.

He placed his hands on her shoulders and turned her around to face him. "Samantha..."

She tried to avoid his eyes. He wouldn't allow it. "Look at me."

She finally did. "What is it?"

He dropped his arms and stared down at her intently. "How long are you going to stay mad at me?"

"How long is eternity?"

"Ah, c'mon, Sam, let's bury the hatchet."

"Good idea," she said acidly. "And I know just *where* I'd like to bury it."

The temptation to strangle her was strong. Instead, Jonathan drove his hands through his hair in an agitated fashion. "Bad choice of words," he admitted. He tried again. "How about a truce?"

"A truce?"

"You know, kiss and make up."

Her stiff formality told him everything he needed to know. "Thank you, anyway, but no thanks."

"Then at least let's be friends. Our job here will be far more pleasant if we quit acting like we can't stand the sight of each other. Besides, people are beginning to talk."

She put her nose an inch higher in the air. "I don't have the vaguest notion what you're talking about."

Jonathan planted himself directly in front of her and hooked his thumbs through his belt loops. "Yes, you do. You're a smart woman. In fact, you're a brilliant woman. Well—" he raised his shoulders and then lowered them again "—maybe not about people. Living people. People who haven't been dead and buried for a millennium or two."

Her eyes squinted with anger. "That was a cheap shot."

"You've been taking cheap shots at me all week," he retorted.

"I have not."

"You have too."

She hesitated, weighing his words. "Well, it's no more than you deserved."

"Maybe not."

That brought her up short.

Jonathan went on. "I want to apologize."

"For what?"

He leaned closer. "For embarrassing you."

"Embarrassing me?"

"The first night we were here. The night I kissed you and you became sexually aroused."

If looks could kill, he'd be dead on the spot.

"I beg your pardon—" she sputtered.

"I'm not going to pussyfoot around the subject any longer, Samantha. Once and for all, we're going to get this thing out in the open."

"No pun intended, right?" she remarked dryly.

Jonathan couldn't help himself. He put his head back and roared with laughter. He even slapped his thigh once or twice. "You see, you *do* have a sense of humor."

"Everyone has a sense of humor."

"The prince doesn't."

A crease appeared between her emerald green eyes. "You're right. I stand corrected. The prince does not have a sense of humor."

His laughter died away, and he was perfectly serious when he said, "I'm going to give it to you straight."

He watched as she raised her eyes upward, indicating the need for patience. Hell, if anyone needed patience, it was him. It took the patience of a bloody saint to deal with the lovely professor.

"The way I see it, Sam, there are two separate issues here. On the one hand, we're supposed to act like we're madly in love with each other as a cover for my job as your bodyguard."

She slanted him a glance. "I thought you weren't my bodyguard."

Jonathan frowned as he folded his arms across his chest. "Let's not argue semantics."

She shrugged her smocked shoulders.

Jonathan picked up the thread of their conversation. "We aren't going to fool anyone if you act like you can't stand the sight of me."

"I can't."

He counted to twenty. Slowly. "Then pretend for the sake of this project."

She sniffed and conceded, "I'll try."

"The other issue is personal." He took a deep breath and plunged ahead. "I find myself very attracted to you. I think you're attracted to me. In fact, I think *that* is what you're really angry about."

"I didn't realize you had a degree in human psychology, *Dr.* Hazard."

"Actually, my advanced degree is in geochemistry," he said offhandedly, "but that doesn't alter the fact that there is something between us, something that doesn't happen every day—certainly not to me and I assume not to you—and you don't like it."

"Poppycock."

"I'll tell you what's pure poppycock, Professor. The damned-fool notion that I became sexually aroused and overcome by lust at the mere sight of the wallpaper." He made a dismissive gesture toward the mural behind them. "It was you, honey. It was kissing you, touching you, feeling you respond to me. That's what turned me on."

She went absolutely still.

Jonathan continued. "I have not found myself in that rather precarious position for a long time, and never with a woman I barely know." At least not since he was an oversexed teenager. "It was you, Sam. It was all you."

Samantha had never thought of herself as a sexy woman.

She was passably attractive, perhaps. She was intelligent, sometimes, even most of the time. But she had never seen herself as a sensual creature, as a creature of the senses.

She was beginning to for the first time in her life. She was even beginning to like the idea...a little. And it was thanks to Jonathan M. Hazard. The credit—or the blame—was his.

She could feel the heat of self-consciousness rising up her neck and spreading onto her face. "I...uh... find you attractive, too, Jonathan."

His expression was solemn. "Thank you, Samantha."

"We will declare a truce."

"An excellent idea."

"We'll attempt to work on this project with a certain degree of harmony and in a spirit of friendship."

"Done." He stuck out his hand. Apparently he expected her to shake it.

Whatever happened to his suggestion of "kissing and making up?"

"Believe me, I'd much rather kiss and make up, too," Jonathan stated as if he had read her mind.

Face burning, Samantha declared, "Let's get to work. We've wasted enough valuable time already."

Nine

"This is going to take forever," Samantha heard Jonathan grumble under his breath as they stood in the doorway of the vast Egyptian storeroom.

"Relax," she said over her shoulder nonchalantly.

She was not feeling in the least bit nonchalant, of course. It wasn't every day that a woman like her found out that a man like Jonathan Hazard couldn't keep his hands off her, that he, in fact, found her irresistible.

She wasn't as immune to masculine flattery as she had always thought, Samantha realized.

"Easy for you to say," the man behind her muttered.

Samantha gave herself a little shake. They were talking about two entirely different things, she reminded herself. "As I said, relax, I'm not going to thoroughly scrutinize the contents," she assured him.

"I assume that means you don't intend to go over each and every object in this room with a fine-tooth comb," he remarked with sarcasm.

"That's exactly what it means. It will take a small army of curators and their assistants to sort, catalog and crate this many artifacts."

"Artifacts?" Jonathan was staring down at several slabs of rotting wood on a long trestle table. "Looks more like plain old junk to me."

"Some of it may appear to be junk to the uneducated eye, but it still has great value to the student and to the scholar. The truly first-rate pieces that Archibald McDonnell acquired have, of course, already been duly recorded and appropriately preserved for posterity."

"Then these are the leftovers."

"In a manner of speaking."

The vast room was piled from floor to ceiling with ancient furniture and household goods, wooden chests, beds and headrests, chairs, chariots, boats and oars, boxes of pottery shards, broken statues, undistinguished canopic jars, wooden shawabtis—miniature servant figures often buried with the mummy—jars, bowls of every size and description, utensils, glazed ceramic tiles, jewelry, kohl containers and bits of rock. There was even a sarcophagus or two.

Samantha reached her hand out and ran a fingertip along the shelf to her right. It came away covered with dirt. "Trout said no one has been in here for several years. I believe him. The dust must be half an inch thick."

"That's odd, then."

"What is?"

Jonathan pointed ahead to a spot where the morning sun was streaming in through a window. It highlighted a section of bare floorboards. "Footprints."

"Footprints?"

"Fresh, too."

Even Samantha could see they had recently been made.

"Obviously they aren't mine and they aren't yours." He went down on his haunches and, rubbing his hand back and forth along his jawline, studied the evidence. "I'd say two sets—one male and one female."

Samantha stared at the floor. "How in the world can you tell?"

One corner of Jonathan's mouth turned up. "Because I'm the expert at this kind of thing, remember?"

She snapped her fingers. "That's right, you are," she said saucily. "You look after the spy stuff, and I take care of the Egyptian part."

"Now you've got it."

"Besides, the heel impressions left in the dust clearly show a pair of men's shoes and a pair of women's."

"How very astute of you, Professor."

She frowned. "I can't imagine why anyone would have been in this storeroom, though."

"Neither can I," Jonathan agreed. Then he added, "I'm not even sure why *we're* in here."

Samantha instilled the same tone of cajolery into her voice that she had heard him recently use. "Ah, c'mon, Hazard, where's your sense of adventure?"

"I forgot to bring it with me."

"What about your curiosity?"

Jonathan patted his shirt pocket and then both the front and back pockets of his jeans. "Funny, I seem to have misplaced it this morning."

"Think of it as the excitement of the unknown, then. The thrill of victory—"

"The agony of defeat," he said drolly.

"What if we were to uncover the archaeological find of the century? Of all time, for that matter?"

He arched a highly skeptical eyebrow in her direction. "If we do, I'll eat my shirt."

"Well, you *do* whatever it is you *do*," she finally suggested. "I'm going to take a look around."

"I'll help," he offered, falling into step behind her. "Are we looking for anything in particular?"

Samantha bent over and studied the dusty items on a dusty shelf. "Not really," she murmured. "If you spot something that seems out of place, something unusual, something that speaks to you, let me know."

"Speaks to me?" Jonathan echoed.

"Don't touch anything, of course," she admonished as they went their separate ways. "It might look like junk to you, but it could be thousands of years old and invaluable to the right researcher."

"Maybe we could just forget the whole thing and throw a big garage sale," Jonathan suggested as he carefully made his way through the roomful of crumbling artifacts.

"These are rather nice," Samantha remarked, gingerly picking up several objects from a nearby shelf.

"What are they?"

"Clappers."

"They look like a pair of hands."

"How very astute of you, Mr. Hazard. Clappers are usually carved of ivory or bone into the shape of a pair of hands and forearms. They were used for ceremonial dances."

"Part of the rhythm section of the orchestra?"

"Exactly."

"What's this?" he inquired, indicating a small, dull-edged implement.

"A razor."

"Must have been tough getting a clean shave with that thing," Jonathan quipped.

"It probably belonged to a woman of the New Kingdom period," Samantha informed him. "Although both Egyptian men and women of that time kept their hair short for cleanliness and for relief from the heat. They wore wigs for festive occasions."

There was one last item on the shelf.

Jonathan backed off, holding his hands up in front of him in mock surrender. "Hey, I'm not even going to ask—"

"It's a fertility symbol, a solid alabaster phallus." Samantha picked the object up and held it firmly in her grasp. "I would say Eighteenth Dynasty, which would make it about three thousand years old. You can see the carvings on the base and here at the very tip." She traced the outline with her finger. "I'd need a magnifying glass to read what it says. No doubt it invokes the names of the various gods and their blessings upon the owner."

Jonathan pulled at the collar of his shirt as if it were suddenly uncomfortably small. "Did I ask?"

It finally dawned on Samantha that Jonathan was embarrassed. His face was even a little ruddy. "Well, it's no worse than the wallpaper," she said, still clasping the stone object in her palm.

"Excuse me, there's an interesting box on the other side of the room," he claimed, and took off.

Samantha shook her head in bewilderment. Men— she would never understand them. Not in a million years. They were a different species altogether.

She returned the alabaster phallus to its place on the shelf and went on to the next storage bin.

A few minutes later, Jonathan called out to her. "Actually, there is an interesting something-or-other over here, Sam. You might want to take a look at it."

"Strange," was her first comment when she saw the pyramid-shaped stone.

"Why strange? It looks like a simple replica of the Great Pyramid."

"It is and it isn't," she told Jonathan, leaning over the table to get a better vantage point. She studied the pyramid from each of its three sides. "It just doesn't make any sense," she muttered.

"What doesn't?"

"See this oval-shaped area?"

"Yes."

"It's called a cartouche. It nearly always encloses the name of a pharaoh or a sovereign."

Jonathan looked expectantly from the model pyramid back to her. "And—?"

"And this cartouche spells out the name of Cleopatra."

"*The* Cleopatra?"

She nodded. "Cleopatra VII Philopator, the one we commonly know as Cleopatra."

"So what's the great mystery?"

"Cleopatra was born in 69 B.C. and committed suicide in 30 B.C."

"The famous asp-in-a-basket trick."

"*Asp* being a generic term. The snake was probably a small cobra." Samantha waved all of that aside with her hand. "That's beside the point. The point is this pyramid was probably carved no earlier than 1870. Maybe 1880."

"Nearly two thousand years after Cleopatra was dead and buried."

"Precisely."

Jonathan shrugged his shoulders. "It's a fake."

"Yes and no."

He turned and stared down at her for a moment. "Did anyone ever tell you, Professor, that there are times when you make no sense at all?"

Samantha tried to explain. "The workmanship is of very poor quality. It's almost as if the artist deliberately tried to make the model ugly. Yet the hieroglyphs are perfectly formed. This was not done by an uneducated man."

"So?"

"It's a gut feeling I have about this pyramid," she admitted.

"Perhaps it's 'speaking' to you."

"Very funny, but there is the science of Egyptology and then there is the art of Egyptology."

Jonathan was suddenly serious. "The great ones always have that extra dimension." They leaned over the low table. He looked from the ugly little pyramid back to her. "What does the artist in you tell you?"

Samantha took in a deep breath and let it out slowly. "It tells me that this was meant to be a disguise."

"A disguise?"

She nodded. "A secret place. A hiding place."

"For what?"

Samantha was about to confess that she didn't know, when a perfunctory knock came on the door of the storeroom, and Martin entered.

"Good morning, Professor. Mr. Hazard."

"Good morning, Martin."

He marched into the room some five or ten feet, came to a halt and snapped the heels of his highly polished black shoes together. "I have been sent to lend a hand."

"Lend a hand?" Samantha repeated. "Sent by whom?"

Martin sighed long-sufferingly. "Mrs. Danvers. She thought you might need someone to fetch and carry for you. I have been volunteered."

"That was very thoughtful of Mrs. Danvers. And of you, Martin," she tacked on diplomatically. "But the truth is that so far there isn't anything to fetch and carry."

The footman's features dropped. "If I can't be of any assistance to you here in the storeroom," he confessed, "I will be assigned to clean the chandelier."

"The gigantic chandelier in the front entranceway with the one thousand light bulbs?"

"The very one," he confirmed.

Samantha tapped a fingernail against her bottom lip. "I'm sure we can find something for you to do, Martin."

His entire face brightened. "Thank you, Professor."

"Just don't touch anything unless I tell you to."

"Of course, Professor. Whatever you say, Professor. I won't move a muscle without your permission, Professor." He took three steps to the right and remained standing at attention, his eyes straight ahead.

"At ease," barked Jonathan.

"Yessir."

Samantha drew Jonathan's attention back to the stone pyramid. "As I was saying—"

The door opened again and a small serving cart was wheeled into the storeroom.

"Refreshments are served," Trout announced. "Tea. Coffee. Freshly squeezed lemonade. A plate of biscuits and small sandwiches for anyone who may have skimped at breakfast. There is also a choice of double-chocolate or lemon cake.''

"What the hell, the more the merrier," Jonathan muttered under his breath.

"Madam thought you might find sorting through dusty whatnots thirsty work."

"That was very kind of Madam," Samantha acknowledged.

"What will you have, Professor?"

"Just a glass of lemonade, thank you." She turned and looked up at Jonathan. "And you, *darling?*"

He stared down at her mouth. They both knew what he *really* wanted.

Samantha cleared her throat. "Mr. Hazard will also have a glass of lemonade, Trout," she said, trying to maintain some semblance of control.

Although the situation in the storeroom was quickly getting out of control.

No sooner had the thought crossed Samantha's mind than she heard another familiar voice ring out.

"My, my, it's positively filthy in here. Why hasn't this room been dusted, Trout? Why hasn't someone seen to it that it was tidied up a bit?"

Trout finished serving them their glasses of lemonade before he replied. "The late master, Mr. McDonnell, absolutely forbid anyone to enter this room, Madam. You may recall that those were always his explicit instructions."

"Yes, I do recall that, now that you mention it." Carlotta sighed and made a production of touching one hand to her head.

It took a minute for Samantha to realize the woman was seeking a compliment about this morning's choice of chapeaus. "What an—unusual hat, Carlotta."

"Thank you, Samantha."

"The squirrel is so lifelike," she added.

"My milliner can do such wonderful things with animals," their hostess exclaimed.

"Milliner or taxidermist?" Jonathan muttered in Samantha's ear. "I always said the lady was a little squirrelly."

"Behave yourself," she warned him under her breath.

Meanwhile, Carlotta was staring down at her feet. It was only then that Samantha realized their hostess was holding two velvet leashes in her other hand. At the end of those velvet leashes were two balls of fawn-colored fluff.

"I must confess that I'm having second thoughts about even allowing Tit and Tat in such a shamefully filthy room," Carlotta crooned.

Tit and Tat?

Samantha swallowed the mouthful of sour lemonade. "I'm not certain this is the place for dogs, anyway."

"Dogs?" sniffed Carlotta.

Samantha quickly backtracked. "You always keep your Pekingese so beautifully groomed. I hate to think of their tiny feet even touching this floor. Let alone their fur dragging along in the dirt and the dust and the grime of years, possibly even of decades.''

"You're absolutely right, of course," the other woman agreed. "This is no place for my precious Tit and Tat."

Samantha breathed a sigh of relief.

But it was too soon.

And it was too late.

She was never able to pinpoint exactly what happened. But the next thing she knew, the velvet leashes slipped from Carlotta's grasp, the dogs were free and chasing each other around the room in a frenzy. Martin tried to grab one and missed. Trout dived after the other and was no more successful.

"Jonathan—?"

He just stood there and swore disgustedly. "What the bloody hell!"

"Madam."

"Trout!"

"Jonathan!"

Carlotta raised her voice above the din. "Tit! Tat! This is very naughty of you."

It all happened in a split second. Samantha watched as the velvet leashes wrapped around and around the table legs. She watched as the already rickety table teetered back and forth. She watched in horror as the stone pyramid went flying through the air. Then it hit the floor of the storeroom and shattered into a thousand pieces.

Ten

SNAFU: Situation Normal All Fouled Up.

They'd had the same problem every now and then when Jonathan had been working for The Company. But he had never witnessed a scene like the one that was unfolding before his eyes.

Barking, yapping little dogs running wild and nipping at everybody's ankles. A woman proudly wearing a stuffed squirrel on her head. An otherwise dignified Englishman diving for an errant Pekingese. A normally cool and calm Samantha screaming his name like a banshee, and all the while digging her fingernails into the flesh on his arm.

The last straw was seeing the stone pyramid he'd discovered, go flying through the air and come down with a resounding crash. It was instantly smashed to smithereens.

Maybe Samantha thought she was in charge of this project. Maybe she considered herself the boss lady. But the situation was getting out of hand and no one appeared in control. Hell, it was already out of control.

It was time he stepped in and took over.

In a voice that had once brought an entire battalion to attention, Jonathan M. Hazard commanded, "Quiet! Everyone quiet down! Now!"

He could have heard a pin drop. Even the damned dogs shut up. It was nice. He rather enjoyed the sensation of being in control, of having that kind of power over people. He'd always known he was a born leader of men . . . and of women, of course.

Then, all of a sudden, Jonathan realized that everyone was staring, mouths agape, at a particular spot on the floor. He marched forward. "What in the—?"

"Good gracious!" gasped Carlotta, her hands clasped to her heaving bosom.

"Holy smokes!" exclaimed Martin.

Trout straightened his tie and admitted, "I have never seen anything quite like it."

"Neither have I," Samantha confessed.

All eyes were on a brilliant triangular gold object sitting upright in the middle of the storeroom floor, surrounded by stone fragments.

It was Samantha who finally announced to the group, "But I think I know what it is."

"*What* is it?" Jonathan asked on their behalf.

"Cleopatra's Pyramid."

"*The* Cleopatra?"

"*The* Cleopatra."

"I've never heard of such a thing," spoke up Carlotta. "Are you sure you don't mean Cleopatra's Needles?"

"Cleopatra's Needles are well-known granite obelisks. One stands in London, the other in New York's Central Park. They are nearly seventy feet tall and weigh over two hundred tons each. No one," he heard Samantha stress, "could possibly mistake Cleopatra's Pyramid for Cleopatra's Needles."

He put in his two cents' worth. "I'm like Carlotta. I've never heard of Cleopatra's Pyramid, either."

"Most people haven't. In fact, many archaeologists and Egyptologists haven't heard of it. The few who have don't even believe in its existence. Throughout the ages, Cleopatra's Pyramid has been regarded as little more than a myth."

"Until now?"

"Until now."

Jonathan was still skeptical. "How can you be certain this is the mythical pyramid?"

"I'm not certain," Samantha told him. "I'll have to take a closer look, examine the construction of the piece and study the hieroglyphs in detail. Once I have the artifact back at the museum, there are a number of experts who can help verify, or disallow, its authenticity." She went a step closer. "Whatever it is—"

Jonathan saw that her skin was covered with goose

bumps "—it's the most beautiful thing I have ever seen."

He had to agree with her. It was beautiful. It appeared to be made of solid gold. It stood approximately twelve inches tall at its peak and twelve inches across at its base. It was covered with strange writing.

Hieroglyphs. The knowledge to read and write the ancient Egyptian script had been lost for several thousand years, only to be rediscovered in the last century, he knew, thanks primarily to the Rosetta stone and a few determined scholars.

"What do you know about Cleopatra's Pyramid?" someone asked Samantha.

"Only a few bits and pieces of the legend," she said. "Queen Cleopatra was supposedly so enamored of the Great Pyramid that she commissioned the finest goldsmith in the land to create one for her in miniature. She requested that it be built to scale. She kept it with her always, and she wanted it to be buried with her. But after her suicide, the gold pyramid disappeared and was never seen again."

"Somebody stole it," proposed Carlotta.

"Very possibly. Grave robbers have been a problem in Egypt since the time of the very first pharaohs and their treasure-rich tombs."

Carlotta gave a sad, little, private laugh. "Do you know what I think?"

"What?"

"I think that poor Archie had no idea what a rare treasure he had in his possession all those years."

"You're undoubtedly right, Carlotta."

Their hostess continued. "No one knows for sure how long the gold pyramid has been hidden under that ugly stone."

"No one knows for sure," Samantha said. "At least a century, perhaps longer."

"Then we have Tit and Tat to thank for discovering what may be the crowning glory someday of the Archibald McDonnell Egyptian Exhibit at the famed Kemet Museum."

"I must confess I hadn't thought of it that way, but your dogs definitely deserve some of the credit."

"Wait until I tell Henry. He's always complaining about my precious Pekingese. Maybe now they'll be treated with the proper respect in this house." The woman made kissing sounds with her pursed pink mouth. "Come along, my sweets. We're off to the kitchen for a special treat." She glanced up at Trout. "Do we have any fillet about the place?"

"Yes, Madam."

"Then Tit and Tat will have fillet for luncheon today."

"As you wish, Madam." The butler looked at the footman. "This has been quite enough excitement for one morning, Martin. It's back to work now."

"Yes, Mr. Trout."

Once they found themselves alone again, Jonathan felt the light touch of Samantha's fingers on his arm. "Would you mind giving me a hand?"

"I'd be delighted to."

"Not that kind of hand."

He tried to appear innocent and failed.

Samantha obviously had more important things on her mind than sex. She lowered her voice to a confidential level. "If this is Cleopatra's Pyramid—and I have a strong hunch that it is—then I want to keep it in my bedroom."

"Why?"

"So I can study it in private. This house is like Grand Central Station, in case you hadn't noticed."

He had noticed.

She pointed to a square piece of plywood slightly larger than the base of the pyramid. "I think if we can transfer the pyramid to that board, we can carry it to my suite."

"We?"

"You."

"That's what I thought." He managed the first part without incident. Then he heaved-ho and picked up both the board and the gold pyramid. "It's fairly heavy, but I don't think it's solid metal," he informed her.

"It doesn't matter." Samantha rubbed her hands together with glee. "I can't wait to get a good look at it. I mean with the proper lighting and my magnifying glass. I'll have to translate the inscriptions, of course. Then examine every minute detail, every square centimeter, every square millimeter." She gazed up at him, her face aglow, and laughed. "I'm rattling, aren't I?"

"Maybe a little."

"Think of it, Jonathan. This could be the archae-ological find of the century. Well, at least since Howard Carter unearthed the treasures of Tutankhamen's tomb.''

''It could be the find of your career.''

''Every Egyptologist, every archaeologist, dreams of finding a special treasure. I don't care how skeptical, how practical they may talk, it's there somewhere in the back of their minds.'' She skipped down the hallway ahead of him and opened the door to the Cleopatra Suite. ''The chances for success are astronomically slim, of course.''

''You'd no doubt have a better chance of winning the lottery.''

''Statistically, I'm sure that's true.''

''Where should I put it?''

''On the desk, I think.'' Samantha hesitated. ''Perhaps the table would be better. Or do you think the bureau?''

''I think it's getting damned heavy, Sam.''

''I'm sorry. Put it on the table, please. Carefully.''

Jonathan set the pyramid down on the table. ''It has already survived one crash landing. We have to assume it was pretty well constructed.''

''Still, I don't want to take any unnecessary risks. I just hope the fall didn't create any cracks or weaknesses.'' She finally seemed to remember his part in the discovery. ''I haven't thanked you yet for drawing my attention to the stone pyramid, Jonathan.''

''It was just a lucky break.''

''A very lucky break as it turned out.''

"Damned if you weren't right about the stone being a disguise." Jonathan shook his head. "Who would have thought?"

"Yes. Who would have thought?"

He twisted his mouth into a sardonic smile. "Does this mean I have to eat my shirt?"

"Nay. Sometime when I need a shirt, you can just give me the one off your back."

"Anytime." And they both knew he meant it. "I'll bet you're chomping at the bit to get a better look at that thing."

"Yes, I am."

"I think I'll make myself scarce for a while."

"Thank you, Jonathan. And thank you for being so understanding," she said; going up on her tiptoes to drop a quick kiss on his mouth.

Hands in his pockets, he paused at the door. "I could always stay and help you."

"You would distract me."

"I could always stay and distract you, then."

"Go away," she scolded. But she was smiling at him all the while.

"I'll come get you for lunch."

"You do that."

But when Jonathan knocked on her bedroom door several hours later and there was no answer, he opened it only far enough to peek around the corner. Samantha was bent over the pyramid, totally engrossed. She had books propped open on every available surface, and page after page of scribbling spread out on the floor around her. Food was the last thing she was interested in.

Jonathan had a tray of sandwiches and fruit brought up and left outside her door. It was still there, untouched, when he walked by to go down for dinner.

The conversation at the dinner table that night was of little else but the gold pyramid and the important part Tit and Tat had played in its discovery. Somehow the meal seemed interminably long to Jonathan without Samantha at the table.

He played billiards with the prince, but his mind wasn't on the game, and Henry beat him fair and square. When Jonathan gave up and went to bed, it was past eleven o'clock. Not a sound came from Samantha's room.

Jonathan undressed and stretched out on his bed. He found himself wondering if Samantha would approach lovemaking with the same single-mindedness, the same concentration, the same passion as she did her work.

If so, a man who spent his nights with the lovely professor might think he had died and gone to heaven.

Eleven

It was after midnight when a discreet knock came on the door of Samantha's bedroom.

Where had the time flown?

That was the first question she asked herself as she stood up, stretched her arms high over her head, rubbed the crick in her neck and stepped over the stacks of books and papers littering the floor.

Who could it be at this hour?

That was the second question Samantha asked herself. Like Little Red Riding Hood—or was it the Three Little Pigs?—she only hoped it wasn't the Big Bad Wolf, or a wolf in sheep's clothing.

She tied the belt of her bathrobe securely around her waist, then went to answer the door. She was certainly presentable and more than modestly attired. She was covered from head to toe. Well, from neck to ankle, anyway.

Her stomach growled insistently. She was hungry. In fact, Samantha suddenly realized, she was starved. She had worked right through lunch and dinner. With any luck, she'd open the door of her suite and it would be Jonathan standing there with a tray of sandwiches, or, at the very least, a plate of cookies and a glass of cold milk.

No such luck.

It was Crispy Green.

"Good evening, my dear," he drawled.

She arched a skeptical eyebrow. "*Evening,* Mr. Green? It is well past midnight."

He didn't act surprised or even bother to consult the expensive gold watch on his wrist. "Is it?"

"Yes, it is." She would have slammed the door in his face, but he was smart enough to have stuck his foot in the crack to prevent that from happening.

"I thought you might be hungry." He had a glass of red wine in one hand and a plate of freshly sliced fruit and cheeses under wrap in the other.

Samantha's mouth began to water.

"No, thank you." She politely but firmly refused the food. She was quite certain there would be strings attached to the late-night offering.

Unpleasant strings.

Crispy's habitually unlit cigar was clenched between his teeth. "Now, honey, I know you must be starved. You missed both lunch and dinner today."

"I frequently skip meals."

"That's not healthy."

"Perhaps not." It also wasn't true, but she would say and do whatever it took to get rid of the man. "When a scientist is hot on the trail of a new discovery, food often has no meaning," she said offhandedly.

Crispy Green's beady eyes brightened. "That's right. I heard you made one hell of a discovery today, with the help of Carlotta's Peks."

"The dogs turned out to be a lucky break."

"A lucky break." Her unwelcome visitor laughed until his more-than-ample abdomen shook like a bowl of gelatin. "Those damn-fool dogs knock over a worthless piece of stone and it breaks apart to reveal a priceless antiquity inside. Lucky break. That is a good one, honey."

"Since I assume you heard the entire story at dinner, Mr. Green—"

Chewing on the end of his stogie, he bellyached, "Lunch *and* dinner. Carlotta recited the whole doggone tale at both meals, along with a few embellishments."

"Then there is nothing for me to add. I am not in the least hungry, but I am very tired. So I will bid you good-night, sir," she stated emphatically and attempted to close the door.

"Looks like my foot's stuck," Crispy Green told her unnecessarily. Then he went on. "As long as I'm here, why don't you invite me in to see this solid gold pyramid of yours, Professor?"

"As I said, Mr. Green, it's late and I'm tired. Perhaps another time."

"You know what they say." He didn't bother to wait for a response from her. "There's no time like the present."

"Believe me, Mr. Green, this is not the time and this is not the place."

"If you won't believe her, then maybe you'll believe me," an extremely annoyed masculine voice spoke up from behind Samantha. "This is not the time and *never* the place, Green."

Jonathan wasn't sure which one of them seemed more surprised—maybe *stunned* was the better word—the weasel wheeler-dealer, or Sam, herself.

The lovely Samantha swung around just as Crispy Green pushed the door of the Cleopatra Suite wide-open. Jonathan knew what they both would see: a man half sitting, half lying across the huge, exotic bed.

He had deliberately propped himself up on an elbow, hair slightly tousled, eyes half-closed, pillows piled up at his back, bedcovers nonchalantly draped across his long legs and pulled up *almost* to his waist.

He was decent.

Barely.

It was obvious that he wasn't wearing a stitch of clothing. And he made no secret of the fact that he wasn't happy about the interruption.

Jonathan rubbed a hand back and forth across his bare chest, then raised his muscular arms above his head and took his own good time yawning and stretching like a man satiated by an evening of exhaustive activity. "It's a little late for a social call, isn't it, Green?"

"Hazard!" The other man choked on his unlit cigar.

"Who'd you expect?" There was a sardonic lift to the dark eyebrows. "Santa Claus?"

"But I thought—"

"What did you think?"

Crispy Green was a shrewd man. He knew there were times when it paid to tell the simple truth. "Frankly, I thought you were staying in the Ramses Room."

"I am." Then Jonathan added with a feral grin, "Off and on."

"I guess I made a mistake."

"I guess you did."

The man was suddenly quite contrite. "I apologize, Professor, for bothering you at this late hour."

"Your apology is accepted," she said regally.

"It won't happen again, will it?" prompted Jonathan.

"It won't happen again," vowed Crispy.

"Just a minute, Green." Jonathan started to get out of bed. "Throw me that towel, will you, honey?"

He watched as Samantha frantically searched for the missing towel. She found it at the foot of the huge bed and tossed it to him like it was a dead snake.

Jonathan whisked the damp towel around his hips as he slipped off the mattress. He sauntered across the room and held out his hands. "The lady may not be hungry, but I seem to have worked up quite an appetite. Thanks for the wine and the snacks.''

Crispy Green blinked. ''You're welcome.''

''Good night.'' Jonathan shoved the door shut with his foot. ''And good riddance,'' he muttered under his breath. Then he turned to Samantha. ''I know you must be nearly faint with hunger. I could hear your stomach growling from across the room.''

''But—''

''Sit. Eat. Then we'll talk.''

Wisely she decided to comply. She sank onto the edge of the bed and dived into the fruit and cheese. Every now and then he would hand her the glass of wine and she took a sip.

''I'm famished,'' she finally admitted, her mouth still full.

''I figured you had to be. You didn't touch any of the food I had left outside.''

She swallowed. ''I wondered about that. I even thought, hoped, prayed it was you with food when I heard the knock on my door a few minutes ago.''

He gave her a stern reprimand. ''Never open your door unless you know who is on the other side.''

Her expression was sheepish. ''I thought it was safe. After all, we're in a private home.''

Jonathan ran his eyes over her for any signs of stress. ''Maybe yes. Maybe no. It depends on who else is in the house.''

''I guess that's true.''

''Of course it's true.''

"Thank you for coming to my rescue," she said, concentrating on a slice of apple.

"You're welcome."

He could see unshed tears poised on the tips of her eyelashes. "Are you hungry?" she suddenly asked. "Would you like some fruit and cheese? There is enough here for both of us."

"Well, maybe just a bite or two." Jonathan dug in.

"There's only the one glass of wine," Samantha said, "but it's too much for me to drink. I'm willing to share, if you are."

"I'm willing to share."

"If you don't want to catch my germs, just turn the glass around and drink out of the opposite side," she told him primly.

Instead, Jonathan deliberately put his mouth on the exact spot where hers had been. The rim of the glass was still warm and steamy from her breath. He glanced up. A drop of wine was clinging to her bottom lip. He leaned forward and, with the tip of his tongue, licked it away.

Samantha's complexion went from ivory to pink to bright red in a matter of seconds. "That was very—"

"Erotic?"

"I was going to say unsanitary."

Jonathan put his head back and laughed.

"I don't see what is so humorous."

"Sam, honey, only last week I had my tongue, my teeth and my mouth all over yours," he said bluntly. "Don't you think it's a little late to worry about germs?"

He noticed it was her habit to change the subject when she became uncomfortable or embarrassed. She did so now. Abruptly. "How did you get in here?"

Jonathan finished chewing the bite of cheese in his mouth, and washed it down with a drink of wine. "In here?"

"In my bedroom."

"Through the door."

Samantha went very still. "Through what door? Crispy Green was blocking the only way in."

He shook his head. "There's another one."

The pitch of her voice raised a full octave. "What do you mean there's another one?"

"I mean there's another door."

"Where?" Her eyes flitted back and forth around the room, from wall to wall, floor to ceiling. "I don't see another door."

"Naturally not."

"Naturally not?"

"It's a secret door."

Samantha lightly slapped her forehead with the palm of her hand. "Of course. How stupid of me. Secret doors. False doors. The ancient Egyptians constructed them all the time."

"This was no ancient Egyptian, but a very clever modern architect."

Samantha stood up. "Where is it?" She raised a hand to stop him. "No. Don't tell me. I want to see if I can find it on my own."

"Okay." Jonathan leaned back against the bedcovers and watched as she began to search the room.

"Am I warm or cold?" she inquired as she approached a section of elaborately painted wall.

How should he know? Then Jonathan realized Samantha was playing a version of the childhood game. "Cold."

She moved to the opposite side of the room. "Now?"

He crossed one bare ankle over the other and popped a piece of papaya into his mouth. "Cold."

"Cold or colder?"

"Colder."

"And now?"

"Cold. Colder. Coldest."

She paused, folded her arms under her breasts and frowned in thought. "There has to be a logical way to go about this."

If there was, Jonathan was certain she would find it. The professor's mind never stopped working. He swore he could almost hear the wheels clicking as they went around and around in her head.

"Where would I put a secret door?" she muttered to herself as she studied the layout of the suite.

Jonathan shrugged his shoulders. "Beats me." He stuffed a bed pillow behind his head and stretched out. He might as well make himself comfortable for the duration. "Do you do this kind of thing very often?"

Samantha was down on her hands and knees, examining the woodwork. "Do what kind of thing?"

"Pig out on midnight snacks. Play silly games. Have pajama parties."

"No. I don't." Her mind was obviously on other things than their conversation.

"Neither do I," Jonathan confessed. "I kind of like it, though. It's fun. Of course," he added after a moment, "I'm not actually wearing any pajamas."

"Neither am I," she admitted.

He choked.

She went on. "I find pajamas very constricting, don't you?"

"Yes."

Samantha had a magnifying glass in her hand now. "I tried a nightgown once. It didn't work, either."

He tried to sound casual. "Whyever not?"

"It kept bunching up at my waist. When I woke up the next morning, the darn thing was wrapped around my neck. Imagine, I was nearly strangled to death by one hundred percent cotton."

Jonathan folded his hands demurely in his lap. He had a very good imagination. Indeed, he had been told that he had an extraordinary imagination.

Unfortunately.

A vivid picture of Samantha's long, lovely, bare legs came to mind . . . all the way up to her waist!

"You've never asked how I knew you were running into trouble with our Mr. Green," he said, as much to divert his own thoughts as hers.

"How did you know?"

"Well, I was just coming out of the shower—" Jonathan decided against mentioning that it was a cold shower and his second of the evening "—when I thought I heard that unmistakably obnoxious laugh of his.''

Samantha shivered. ''The sound of it sends chills down my spine.''

''I couldn't imagine what business Crispy Green would have in this wing of the house at twelve-fifteen in the morning, so I decided to take a look-see.''

Samantha glanced over at him. ''A look-see?''

''It's technical jargon used by us professionals. It means to examine, to inspect, to investigate, to snoop, to stick one's nose in where it doesn't belong.''

''In other words, you were spying on me.''

Jonathan blew out his breath expressively. ''That's about the size of it.''

''Thank God you were!'' Samantha exclaimed. ''I'm not sure I could have gotten rid of him. The man does not know how to take no for an answer.''

Jonathan knew his eyes had grown darker and his lips thinner. ''What part didn't he understand? The N or the O?''

''Crispy Green isn't the only one with the problem. A lot of men don't seem to understand a simple no.''

''Is that the reason you've stayed away from men?''

''It's one of them.'' Then she clapped her hands together and jumped up and down with excitement. ''I've found it! I've found it, Jonathan! Your secret door!''

Twelve

"**H**ow did you figure it out?" he asked her.

"It was very simple really," Samantha explained, pushing her glasses up on her nose. "It was the row of light switches by the door. You will notice that there is a switch for each fixture or lamp in the room—" she paused for dramatic emphasis "—and *one* left over." She didn't like to gloat, but it was a brilliant piece of detective work. "I deduced that the extra light switch must operate the secret panel or door."

Jonathan smiled down at her and even gave her a pat on the back. "Elementary, huh, my dear Watson?"

She flipped the last switch and they watched as a seamless section of the wall between their two rooms slowly swung open. "Voilà!"

"Very good, Professor."

Samantha grinned from ear to ear. "Thank you, Mr. Hazard." She was curious. "How did you discover the secret door?"

"We were taught at spy school to always check out light bulbs, switches, lamps, electrical appliances—"

"Toasters? Coffeepots?"

"You never know where you might uncover a hidden microphone, a surveillance camera, a miniature transmitter, that kind of thing," he said matter-of-factly.

"The spy business must have been very high tech even in your day."

"Yes, it was very high tech *even* in my day." Then Jonathan scowled. "Somehow you make me sound like I'm past my prime."

"How old are you?"

Another scowl creased his forehead. "What does age have to do with being in your prime?"

"Actually, very little."

"I'm thirty-six and just hitting my stride," he informed her.

Samantha considered the relative question of age. "Thirty-six is too old, perhaps, to be gallivanting about the world playing James Bond, but young by almost any other standard."

"Exactly."

"Nevertheless, this might not be the time to take up professional tennis or Olympic swimming."

"I have no intentions of doing either one," he said.

"Then there is the field of gymnastics where puberty seems to be the dividing line," she observed.

"You don't have to elucidate any further, Sam. I get the point. While we're on the subject, how old are you?"

Samantha blinked owlishly. "Are you allowed to ask a lady that question in this day and age?"

"Hey, turnaround is fair play, Professor."

"You're absolutely right." She squared her shoulders. "I'm twenty-nine."

"I knew it!"

She uttered an impatient noise. "Well, if you already knew my age, why did you ask?"

"I didn't know your age."

"You just said you did."

Jonathan threw his arms up in the air in a gesture of utter futility. "That's what I mean."

"What?" she demanded to know.

"There is a basic communication problem between men and women. We do not speak the same language."

Samantha quickly jumped to the defense of all womankind. "Is it any wonder? We're not the same sex. I'm not even certain we're the same species, and there are times when I wonder if we come from the same planet."

They both calmed down.

"What, do you suppose, brought on that little tirade?" he asked.

"Yours or mine?"

Jonathan began to laugh. Samantha decided to join in.

Somewhere in the midst of all the hilarity, she was reminded that it was the middle of the night, that she was in the intimacy of her bedroom, that she was wearing only a pair of skimpy undies under her bathrobe and that the handsome and virile male next to her had nothing more than a damp towel hitched around his hips. A damp towel that could easily slip and fall to the floor at any moment, leaving them both in a most embarrassing and revealing situation.

How did a woman delicately suggest to a man that he put on his pants?

Samantha cleared her throat awkwardly. "Perhaps it's time you . . . ahem . . ."

"Left?"

That caught her off guard. "Are you leaving?"

"Do you want me to leave?"

"Do you want to leave?"

Jonathan raised his index fingers in the shape of the letter T. "Time out!"

"Now what?"

"It's starting all over again, Samantha."

"What is?"

She heard him heave an exaggerated sigh. "Misunderstanding each other." He paced the room. "What we need are a few simple guidelines."

"A few simple guidelines," she repeated.

" 'Say what you mean.' "

" 'And mean what you say.' "

He stopped in front of the open doorway between their two bedrooms. "We will attempt to speak in concise language whenever possible."

"Concise language."

"We will tell each other only the truth."

"Only the truth."

"We will not play games."

Samantha's face fell.

"Okay, we can play games," Jonathan hastily amended. "But only if we both know what game we're playing, when we're playing it and we agree on the rules ahead of time."

"Oh, good grief!"

"I don't think I know that one," he admitted. But Samantha caught the twinkle in his eye.

"I want you to be serious for a minute," she told him. His handsome face instantly sobered. "Jonathan, are you going back to your own room tonight?"

"If you want me to."

She spoke without looking at him. "What if I don't know?"

"Then we have a problem."

Samantha felt submerged in double meanings. "Do you want to stay?"

"Yes."

That was simple enough.

He went on. "I'd like to crawl into that big bed with you and hold you in my arms. I'd like to kiss you, touch you, make love to you."

"Sex."

"It's a lot more than sex at my age."

"Mine, too," she confessed. Her heart began to pound in her ears. "Sometimes you scare me, Jonathan."

"There are times when you scare the living hell out of me, too."

Her voice softened. "You make me feel safe, safer than I have ever felt before."

"I want to keep you safe, Sam. I want to take care of you. I want to make sure that guys like Crispy Green never get within a mile of you. It makes my blood boil when I think about scum like that anywhere near my—" his voice caught "—anywhere near a woman like you."

There was silence for a minute or two.

Then she moistened her bottom lip and told him, "You make me happy."

"I'm glad to hear that," Jonathan purred.

"You also make me sad."

"I know."

"One minute I'm thrilled to be with you, and frankly, the next I would gladly throttle you if I could."

Jonathan expelled a breath of indulgent laughter. "You know what it's called, don't you, sweetheart?"

Samantha wasn't sure she wanted to hear what he had to say. "What is it called?"

"L-O-V-E," he spelled out.

"I—I can't be in love with you," she retorted. "And you certainly can't be in love with me."

Strong, masculine hands were settled on towel-clad hips. "Why not?"

Why not!

The notion of their being in love with each other was too ridiculous to even entertain. It was crazy. It was insane. It was plain stupid.

Cool and calm as you please, Samantha told him, "To begin with, we have only known each other for a week and a day."

"Some people believe in love at first sight," Jonathan observed.

"Well, I'm not one of them. I don't believe you are, either. We're practical people, Jonathan. We're well educated, well traveled professionals. We aren't a couple of impressionable teenagers. We know that a real relationship is built upon mutual respect, common goals and similar interests."

His eyebrows rose fractionally. "I happen to respect you very much."

"And I respect you." She did, too. Perhaps more than any man she had ever met.

"I want a family, a home and a fulfilling career. Isn't that what you want?" he said obstinately.

"I suppose so."

If she were honest with herself, Samantha knew she had never gone beyond planning her career. She had always assumed there would be plenty of time for the rest later.

When was *later?* What if *later* was now? What if *later* never came?

"We're opposites," she argued in desperation.

"They say opposites attract," he countered.

"*They* say a lot of things. That doesn't necessarily make them true." She thought for a minute or two. "What are our similar interests? What do we have in common?"

"We each have our own interests and we can learn to enjoy each other's. I know a couple where she has learned to play golf and he goes to the opera. And he hates opera."

She persisted. "I don't know the first thing about you."

Jonathan came right back with, "Yes, you do. You know what kind of man I am fundamentally. You may not know all the details yet, but finding out is half the fun."

Samantha blurted out the cruelest truth of all. "But you drive me nuts!"

He threw his arms up in the air in a gesture of triumph. "It's a sure thing, then. Because *you* drive *me* nuts!"

"You're crazy."

He lowered his arms. "Okay, don't call it love if the word bothers you. Call it infatuation. Call it sexual attraction. Call it basic human curiosity. All I know is I want you, and you want me."

Samantha opened her mouth, intending to call him a liar. Then she realized it was true. She did want him.

Jonathan took a step closer, but he still didn't touch her. "If you say no, Samantha, then I'll know you mean no. And I will walk out of this room and not come back."

Dear God!

Jonathan put it plain and simple. "Yes or no?"

She threw her arms around his neck. "Yes!"

"I don't remember ever wanting a woman the way I want you," he vowed, gazing down into her eyes.

"I have never desired a man as I desire you, Jonathan. Let's make love all night long."

He laughed. "Oh, honey, if only we could."

"Can't we?"

"We sure can try," he promised her.

"What about the little 'necessities?' " Samantha inquired as delicately as she could. She might be inexperienced but she wasn't dumb.

"They have been provided by the same wise and thoughtful host who supplied the bathroom with toothbrush, toothpaste, soap, deodorant and shaving cream. All the conveniences of home, in fact."

There was an awkward moment or two.

Samantha finally confessed, "I don't know where to start."

"We can start wherever we like," Jonathan said to her. "There aren't any hard-and-fast rules, honey. We can have more wine and cheese. We can sit cross-legged on the floor and tell each other all about our childhoods. We can play pinochle until dawn. We can—"

Sometimes men talked too much.

"Jonathan—"

"Yes, Samantha."

"Shut up and kiss me."

This time there was no hesitation; there were no second thoughts. The moment his mouth touched hers, Samantha knew it was right. This was the right time and the right place—and most important—the right man.

"You have beautiful hair, glorious hair," he whispered to her as he tugged at the combs and hairpins that held it in place.

They went flying in every direction. Her hair came tumbling down, cascading around her shoulders, covering his hands, his arms, his chest. Jonathan seemed to delight in burying his face in the thickness of it, in inhaling her scent, in tasting her skin.

She drove her fingertips through his short, dark hair and made an amazing discovery of her own. "It's so soft," she said with wonderment. "I had no idea it would feel like silk."

"Silk." His voice vibrated with the word.

She traced a path from his hairline to his eyebrows—they were dark, emphatic, yet nicely arched—across the bridge of his nose, around each well-shaped ear and back to his mouth.

"I like your mouth, Jonathan Hazard."

"I like yours, Samantha Wainwright."

She tossed her glasses down on the bedside table behind them. "I like the way your mouth looks. I like the shape of it. I like the feel of it. I like the way it tastes. The way you taste."

Samantha went up on her tiptoes and kissed him, softly at first, even a little tentatively. As she gained confidence, she became more daring. She teased and tantalized and tormented him with the tip of her tongue until he opened his mouth and devoured hers in an impassioned kiss that left her with no breath, no backbone and no brain.

"How can that be, Jonathan?"

"How can *what* be?"

"I consider myself an intelligent woman. Yet you kiss me and all of a sudden I can't seem to string two words together. I can't come up with a single coherent thought."

"It's time to stop thinking and start feeling, darling."

"It feels so good," she groaned, his breath hot and sweet and insistent.

"It's only going to get better," he promised her.

"I don't believe you." Yet she shivered as he dragged his lips along her neck and across her shoulder where he had pushed aside her bathrobe.

"Believe me," Jonathan said in a husky voice, his breath coming quicker and hotter, his hands more sure as they found the tie around her waist.

He tugged at her robe and Samantha was vaguely aware that it slipped from her shoulders and pooled around her feet. Suddenly, she wished she were wearing something more feminine, more alluring than her usual plain cotton underwear.

"If I had known where this was going to lead to, I would have gone out and bought something satin, something sexy, maybe in red or black," she murmured against his mouth.

"You're sexy as hell just the way you are," Jonathan insisted, pressing her hips against his.

Samantha could feel him jutting out against the towel. He was already fully hard.

The rest was accomplished without fanfare and without embarrassment. Jonathan unhooked the back of her bra and slid her panties off. Then he unhitched the damp towel from around his hips and tossed it aside. They stood there by the exotic bed, the diaphanous curtains swaying all around them, and looked at each other for the first time.

"You are beautiful," he said, and reached out, cupping the fullness of her breasts in his hands. "You are even more than I had hoped for or dreamed of." Then he circled her nipples with his thumbs, and she shivered from head to toe.

"You're beautiful, too, and you're very big," Samantha said, gazing down at that part of him that needed no introduction and apparently no encouragement.

His manhood was smooth and hard, and appeared to be nestled in a tangle of dark curls. As she watched, it moved and twitched. It seemed to take on a life of its own. She found herself fascinated by it.

"You can touch me if you wish," Jonathan said tightly.

"May I?"

"Absolutely."

So she did.

It was wonderful. *He* was wonderful. Jonathan was the most fascinating paradox she had ever encountered. His body was all soft flesh and hard muscle. He was tall and strong—many times stronger than she could ever be—yet he was utterly and completely at her mercy when she caressed him.

She ran her hand up and down the silky shaft. She traced the length and breadth of him with her thumb. She gently flicked the opening with her fingernail.

She was even more intrigued by Jonathan's reaction to her touch. He swayed a little unsteadily as if it set him back on his heels. There was a fine line of perspiration on his upper lip and another across his forehead.

She was concerned. "Are you all right?"

"Never been better," he claimed.

She tried to fan his face with her free hand. "Are you warm or something?"

"Hot is more like it," he insisted, and managed to laugh at his own joke.

When it seemed that Jonathan could stand no more, he reached for her again. He bent his head and touched her breast with the tip of his tongue, flicking it back and forth across her now-sensitized nipples. Samantha could feel the erotic pull all the way down to her toes.

Jonathan said one word, "More." Then he took her into his mouth and suckled, drawing her in deeper and deeper, nipping on her tender flesh, erotically tugging at her, until her head fell back and a low moan issued forth through her parted lips.

"Jonathan, help me!" she cried out, gasping.

His head flew up. "What is it?"

"I—I can't seem to stand up," she told him, bewildered. "My legs won't support me."

"Then we need to lie down," he said as if it was a totally reasonable suggestion. "And there just happens to be a bed right behind us."

He took her by the hand and stretched out alongside her on the mattress.

It seemed like an obvious thing to say, but Samantha said it, anyway. "We're different."

"Very. Or as the French would say, *'Vive la différence!'*" Jonathan confirmed as they explored all the *différences* between them.

"And yet we fit together perfectly."

"It's a damned miracle."

"It is, isn't it?"

"Yes."

She could feel his touch on her stomach, then lower to the soft womanly mound and the tangle of strawberry blond curls, and finally, between her legs, dipping and delving into the very female heart of her.

Her reactions were instinctive and utterly natural. Her hips came off the bed. Her hands clasped his shoulders, her nails unknowingly scraped his flesh. She urged him closer. She wanted him closer. She needed him closer.

There was a gentle probing in the beginning, then even more insistent movement, and finally she felt Jonathan inside her. He thrust into her again and again, farther, stronger, harder, deeper.

She could not think; she could only feel.

Lovemaking.

Eternity.

The past, the present, the future: they became one.

Thirteen

"**B**y the way, have you seen my etchings?"

Samantha laughed softly. It was a joyous sound. Jonathan could feel her warm, sweet body moving next to his as she curled up in the crook of his arm. "I didn't know that line was still in use."

God, she was good! Making love was good. In fact, it was great, Jonathan corrected himself. He had never felt better in his whole damned life.

He gazed down at her. "It's no line. There are etchings covering the ceiling of my bedroom. I've been staring at them every night for hours."

Samantha craned her neck and looked at him. A small crease appeared between her emerald green eyes. "You've been staring at them?"

He paused and then told her in a different voice, "Studying them. I've been studying them."

"That's not what you said. You said *staring* at them." She arched one blond eyebrow. "'A few simple guidelines. Say what you mean and mean what you say. Speak concisely. Tell only the truth.'"

It had been his idea. Those were his exact words. She was only quoting to him what he'd said.

"Okay, I've been staring at them," Jonathan admitted. "I don't understand their meaning. Strange-looking animals. Cows and ducks lined up like pigeons in a shooting gallery. A bunch of hieroglyphs I can't read." He sighed melodramatically. "I'll bet they tell a wonderful bedtime story."

Samantha chuckled in the back of her throat. It was an utterly feminine little sound. Jonathan found he liked it. A lot.

"Would you like to show me your etchings?" she finally said.

"I thought you'd never ask," he drawled.

It was sometime later before they actually got around to studying the drawings on the ceiling of the Ramses Room. First, they made love again. This time in his bed.

"I wonder what those figures represent?" he said, pointing toward a section of the illustration.

Her eyes followed the direction of his raised arm. "They look like the gods of the Nile flood holding Egypt's riches."

"Huh?"

"Egypt was—is—called 'the Gift of the Nile.' The country could not exist without the river. The Nile has always given Egypt its water, its rich farmland, its very existence."

"The River of Life."

"Exactly."

While lying flat on his back, Jonathan inquired tongue-in-cheek, "Have you noticed, Professor Wainwright, the frequent and explicit use of phallic symbols in ancient Egyptian art?"

"Yes."

He showed his white teeth in a wicked smile. "To what do you attribute this phenomenon?"

"Sex."

He made a fist and pretended to stick a microphone under her nose. "Would you care to delve into that a little deeper for me, Professor?"

"Certainly."

"What about erotic papyri?"

"I think you will find that the preferred form of the plural, according to Webster's, is papyruses," she said with what sounded suspiciously like a giggle.

"Whatever you say, Professor. You're the expert."

"No. But I could be with practice," she murmured meaningfully.

Jonathan felt a path of moist kisses being trailed along his chest, and the arrowed tip of a tongue flicking back and forth over first one of his nipples and then the other. The thought crossed his mind that he may have created a monster. "Think of it for a moment, if you will."

"I already am," she confessed.

He made a disparaging sound. "I am speaking of phallic symbols."

"So am I."

He gave an example. "Cleopatra's Needle."

"The tall, slender shape of the obelisk," she expounded on his behalf.

"The Pyramids of Giza."

"The last surviving wonder of the Seven Wonders of the ancient world. Their incredible size can scarcely be conceived until one is standing before them."

Jonathan quirked a dark eyebrow. "Seeing is literally believing, then?"

"It has certainly made a believer out of me," the slender woman beside him stated. But he noticed that her gaze was *not* on the ceiling.

He named another possibility. "The great temples of Luxor and Karnak."

"Huge columns spearheaded toward the heavens, themselves." Samantha began giving him more symbolic examples with surprising enthusiasm and originality. "The king's specter. The headdress of Amun. The familiar palm tree growing beside the river. The colossal figures at Abu Simbel."

"Apparently the list is endless," he said dryly.

"My personal favorite is the Great Pyramid," she confided, moving her hand down his torso.

Jonathan had to know. "Why is that?"

"No words or pictures can prepare you for your first sight of it."

He blinked. "I see."

"It is legendary. It is mysterious. It is immense."

He took her comments as a personal compliment. "Thank you."

"You're welcome." Rather shyly Samantha said to him, "There is more."

Jonathan had never been compared to the Great Pyramid before. He found it a most unusual—and exhilarating—experience. "By all means, please continue."

So she did. "It has an unexpected opening, a narrow tunnel and a great treasure inside."

He choked on his saliva.

Samantha gave him a helpful pat on the back. "Are you all right?"

He pulled her across his body and cupped her bare bottom in his hands. "I will be."

It was just before dawn when Samantha was aware of Jonathan dropping a languorous kiss on her mouth, muttering something about taking a shower, then slipping out of bed.

Sleep had been minimal. But it was, without a doubt, the best night of her entire life.

Burrowing down into the bedcovers, Samantha lay there in that wondrous dream state between waking and sleeping. Seemingly random thoughts drifted in and out of her consciousness.

The Great Pyramid.

"Your eyes are the color of rare emeralds."

"The Cleopatra?"

Rare emeralds.

"So much for the disguise."

"It's a secret door."

"Where would I put a secret door?"

It was a brilliant piece of detective work.

"Cleopatra VII. The one we commonly know as Cleopatra."

A secret place. A hiding place.

The Great Pyramid.

Samantha's eyes flew open; she was suddenly wide awake. She pushed herself up onto her elbows. Her heart was beating in double time. Ideas were spinning around and around in her head. Questions were raised faster than she could answer them.

But one thought kept niggling at her.

Why had the miniature gold pyramid been created in the first place?

Had it been made merely as a decoration? A beautiful object to be admired? A fancy whatnot to sit on a table or a chest or, perhaps, beside Queen Cleopatra's bed?

Or had it served some purpose, some useful function?

And if so, as *what?*

Samantha hopped out of bed and reached for the nearest article of clothing. It was Jonathan's shirt. She slipped it on, discovering it buttoned modestly to midthigh.

"Jonathan?" The water was running in the shower. He couldn't hear her call his name.

She dashed into the adjoining bedroom, grabbed a pair of her cotton panties from the bureau drawer and pulled them on. "Good enough," she said of her makeshift outfit.

She picked up her glasses—she always concentrated better when she was wearing them—pulled up a chair and plunked herself down in front of the gold pyramid.

"What is your secret?" she asked out loud, carefully studying the centuries-old artifact.

It was an amazing piece of workmanship, Samantha reflected. She was convinced—had been convinced from the beginning—that this was the genuine article. It was an exact replica of the huge stone pyramid built two thousand years before Cleopatra had lived and died.

Since childhood, Samantha had been aware of the numerous legends surrounding the Great Pyramid. As the daughter of an Egyptologist, they were her fairy tales. There was the one about the undiscovered sarcophagus of the pharaoh, still lying buried in a hidden chamber deep within the pyramid.

There was another about the precise mathematical measurements and their mystical significance, at least according to some. Then there were the stories of the caliph who had rediscovered the entrance to the Great Pyramid in the ninth century while searching for an emerald of mythical proportions.

There was not one story she didn't know by heart.

"What do your instincts, what does your heart, tell you now, Samantha?" she whispered as she ran her fingertips over the smooth surface of gold.

A secret place. A hiding place.

"Where would I put a secret door?"

"I know where," she speculated out loud. "I'd put it where the original door was located."

She quickly looked around her on the bedroom floor for the book she'd been reading earlier on the Great Pyramid. She found it, picked it up, nervously flipped through its pages and read the passage she was searching for:

Those who built the Great Pyramid tried to out-wit ancient grave robbers by placing the entrance to the pharaoh's tomb twenty-four feet east of the middle and fifty-five feet above the base. Then they covered it with a single slab of stone cut into the surface. That way, the opening was invisible from below.

"Twenty-four feet from the middle," she muttered, "and fifty-five feet above the base. Now, if the replica was built on a scale of..." She scribbled her calculations on a scrap of paper and came up with an answer.

The answer, she told herself.

It was time to put her theory to the test. Using a mathematician's ruler, she measured from both the base and the side of the miniature pyramid. She located the exact spot and carefully pressed with the tip of her pen.

Nothing happened.

She tried again, pressing a little harder.

Nothing.

Maybe she was wrong. Maybe she didn't have the answer, after all.

There is the science of Egyptology and there is the art of Egyptology.

Samantha knew in her heart of hearts that she was right. She decided to try one more time.

Carefully positioning the point of the pen, she pushed against the pyramid's surface. Something seemed to move, to give. She gave another push, and then another.

A small drawer popped out.

There was something inside it. She put the pen down and raised her hand. She was trembling with excitement, shaking like a leaf.

She took in a deep, steadying breath and slowly let it out. Then she reached into the drawer and removed what appeared to be a very old cloth pouch. Carefully opening the top, she peeked inside.

They were shiny.

They were green.

Samantha emptied the contents of the pouch onto the table. "Ohmigod!"

They were emeralds.

Stunned, she sat there for a moment without moving, without speaking. Then she jumped to her feet. "I've got to tell Jonathan," she cried out softly.

"I don't think so, Professor," came an icy cold voice from behind her as the ice-cold barrel of a gun was pressed into her back.

Fourteen

"Samantha?"

There wasn't any answer.

Jonathan hitched a towel around his hips—it was getting to be a habit—and padded out of the bathroom.

She wasn't in his bed.

The secret door between the Ramses Room and the Cleopatra Suite was, however, standing wide open. He sauntered across and called her name again. "Samantha?"

There was no answer.

It had been a long time, but Jonathan realized he was starting to get a bad feeling about this whole thing, an unpleasant sensation in his gut, a little pinprick of warning that niggled at the back of his neck.

He walked into Samantha's bedroom. The room was empty. The bed was empty. She was nowhere in sight.

"Son of a—" Jonathan spiked his fingers through his still-wet hair.

He had to keep a cool head. He had to think clearly. Act intelligently. Analyze objectively. He couldn't afford to jump to conclusions. He had to consider his options.

Details were noted dispassionately. Samantha's eyeglasses were gone from the bedside table. A bureau drawer, filled with cotton underwear, was partially ajar. Her bed was exactly as it had been left several hours earlier. There were no visible signs of a struggle.

Jonathan turned and spotted the gold pyramid on the table. He examined the small secret drawer—it was no secret anymore, of course—the scrap of paper with calculations scribbled all over it, the specialized ruler, the pen.

The lovely professor had been up to something. It even appeared as if she'd found something.

What?

All the years of training came back to Jonathan in a rush. All of his instincts were on red alert. Samantha was in trouble. Big trouble. He just knew it. He had to move fast. Time was of the essence.

He turned on his heel and stalked back to his own room. The towel was unceremoniously dropped to the floor. He grabbed his jeans and pulled them on, noting that his shirt was missing. Then he opened the bottom drawer of the bureau, dived beneath a pile of socks and brought out his gun. It was a small, compact Beretta. He double-checked the clip, made sure the safety was on and slipped the weapon into the waistband of his denims.

Barefooted and bare-chested, Jonathan flipped off the lights and silently opened the door of the Ramses Room. He glanced to his right and to his left.

Nothing.

No one.

He stepped into the hallway and, without a sound, closed the door behind him. Moving from shadow to shadow, he worked his way along the corridor. He had nearly reached the top of the grand staircase when he heard someone coming.

He quickly faded into a dark corner and waited, his palm resting lightly on the handle of the Beretta.

"There's something fishy going on around here," came the quiet mutter.

Jonathan dropped his voice to just above a whisper. "Trout?"

The butler froze on the spot. "Is that you, Mr. Hazard?" he replied in kind.

A softly hissed, "Yes."

The Englishman peered into the inky blackness. "Where are you?"

"Five paces straight ahead, then two to your left."

"My word," mouthed Trout, "I didn't see you until this very instant, sir."

"That was the idea," Jonathan said dryly.

Trout lowered his head and confided, "I don't wish to seem an alarmist, but something is amiss in this house tonight, Mr. Hazard."

"You can say that again."

"You noticed it as well, then?"

Jonathan nodded. "You might say so."

He could make out enough of the other man's features to see the recognition on them when the butler finally put two and two together and came up with four.

"Ah . . . that no doubt explains why you are slinking about the hallways at three o'clock in the morning, half-dressed, still dripping from your bath and carrying a rather nasty-looking pistol in your pants, sir."

"No doubt it does."

Trout brandished the stick in his hand. "I have a weapon with me, as well."

Jonathan arched a quizzical eyebrow. "Weapon?"

"In the right hands, a most formidable weapon," he said with confidence. "It is my old cricket bat."

"Good show. Now let's get down to business." Jonathan took a breath and let it out quietly. "Samantha—Professor Wainwright is missing."

Trout frowned. "She's not in her room?"

"No."

"That is something of a coincidence."

"Why?"

"I was roused from my sleep some while ago by a noise—I confess I don't know exactly what kind of noise. Anyway, as is my custom under such circumstances, I began to double-check the house. I discovered that both Mrs. Danvers and Martin are not in their quarters."

"I'll bet Crispy Green isn't in his room, either," Jonathan gambled.

"Normally I would not speak ill of any guest in this house," Trout said by way of a preamble.

"Naturally not."

"After all, it's not my place to pass judgment on my employers' guests or friends."

"I understand."

"Nevertheless—"

"Go on. Go on, man," Jonathan urged.

"I have my suspicions concerning Mr. Green."

Jonathan realized he sounded almost savage. "That makes two of us."

"I do not think he is a gentleman."

"I think you're absolutely right."

"I believe that Mr. Green has pulled the proverbial wool, so to speak, over the prince's and Madam's eyes."

It wouldn't take much to accomplish that, Jonathan thought to himself.

"Indeed—" Trout was quite agitated now "—I am very much afraid that Mr. Green may be of the criminal class."

"I have the same fear," admitted Jonathan.

"Do you think he has the professor in his evil clutches?"

Jonathan went cold on the inside. "Yes. I do."

"Where do you suppose they are?"

"I don't know for certain. But I have a pretty good hunch."

"A hunch, sir?"

"I have a good idea where they are, and I think it's because Samantha found something."

"What?"

He shrugged his bare shoulders. "I suspect it was an object hidden in the gold pyramid. My guess is that it's very old, very Egyptian and very valuable."

"So where would you abscond to with something very old, very Egyptian and very valuable?" Trout pondered.

"The Egyptian storeroom," they said in unison.

Trout nodded and rubbed his palms together. "The game's afoot, ay?"

"This is no game, Trout."

"Of course not, sir." He snapped to attention, raising his cricket bat. "What is your plan?"

"My plan?"

"You have a plan, of course. We cannot go riding in, pistols blazing, bullets flying every which way, like your American cowboys. Someone could get hurt."

"Samantha."

"Yes, the professor."

Jonathan stood very still for a moment. Then he turned to his companion. "Can you act?"

Trout blinked. "I beg your pardon."

"Have you ever done any acting?" he said, carefully enunciating each word.

There was a snigger from the butler. "Surely you jest."

"I guess not," Jonathan concluded.

"*Au contraire*, Mr. Hazard. Every good butler is a superb actor. Indeed, he *must* be." Trout lowered his voice another tone on the scale. "I will tell you a little secret. You once asked how I was able to accurately predict the size of clothing and footwear you required."

"Yes."

"I learned it from my father."

"Was he a tailor?"

"No, indeed, sir. He was an entertainer."

"An entertainer!"

"He and my dear mother were a song-and-dance team. They taught me everything I know. When I first went out on my own at the age of fourteen, I worked the seashore. I would take my hat off and put it down in front of me on the dock. Then I would sing and dance, perform magic tricks, recite poetry and bits of famous plays, guess the height, or weight, or sometimes the age of those on holiday. I did whatever it took to fill my hat with coins. That is how I made my living."

"Amazing."

"I have done everything theatrically from silly, suggestive limericks to rather good Shakespeare, if I do say so myself," he confided to Jonathan.

Jonathan was dead serious. "What I need is a diversion."

Trout gave an emphatic nod. "Then you shall have a diversion, sir."

"Here is what I want you to do..." He outlined a plan to his companion. Then after a moment, Trout went in one direction and he in another.

Jonathan slipped silently through the night toward the light he could see was on in the storeroom. All of his skills, all of his instincts had to be functioning at their peak efficiency in the next few minutes. Samantha's life might well depend on them, on him.

Rage tore through Jonathan.

Icy cold rage.

Somebody would pay the price if even one hair on the lovely Samantha's head were harmed.

And the price would be high, indeed.

The night was warm, but Samantha was cold. She shivered and tried to think.

Three against one. The odds were definitely not in her favor. Besides, someone—probably the ever-efficient Mrs. Danvers—had suggested that they tie her hands behind her back.

For the time being, Samantha decided to sit quietly in the corner where they had left her and listen. Perhaps something would come to her, some way to escape, some plan to save herself.

Perhaps Jonathan would come.

Her heart contracted painfully at the prospect. She had no way of warning Jonathan of the danger he would walk into if he came through that door looking for her.

He mustn't come for her. He must stay away. She squeezed her eyes tightly shut and concentrated on the thought. She was interrupted by an argument between her captors.

"I thought I told you to bring me the gold pyramid," Crispy Green complained, chomping on the end of his cigar.

Martin wrung his hands in nervous agitation. "There was a door open between the professor's room and Hazard's. I could hear the water running in the shower. He might have come out any second. I couldn't take a chance. Maybe you want to tangle with the man, but I don't."

Mrs. Danvers stepped forward and partially shielded the footman with her matronly body. "You've been after us to find something of value to pay off Martin's debt. Well, all right, here you are, Mr. Green. Here is a bag of precious emeralds that cannot be identified and cannot be traced. There are no distinguishing marks. No history. No background. No records." She made a gesture toward Samantha. "The girl is probably the only living human being who even knows they exist."

Samantha's heart sank.

Mrs. Danvers was a fool. It would have been far better if that fact had *not* been pointed out to Crispy Green. The truth was, three people besides the odious toad, knew about the emeralds—which made Mrs. Danvers and Martin as expendable as herself.

"You've got a point," the man admitted, twirling the large diamond ring around and around on his pinkie. "I can turn emeralds into cold, hard cash with a lot less hassle than a one-of-a-kind gold pyramid."

"I've heard that the black market for emeralds is simply teeming with eager buyers and sellers, dealers who don't ask too many questions, intrigue and smuggling. No one will know and no one will care where these emeralds came from," said the ever-informative housekeeper.

Martin jerked his head in Samantha's direction. "What are we going to do with her?"

Crispy leered. "I know a couple of things *I* wouldn't mind doing with the lovely professor."

Samantha's skin crawled.

Crispy took a step toward her and caressed her cheek with the back of his smooth, white hand. She flinched. "As lovely as the professor is, she's of no use to me. You weren't supposed to bring her," he grumbled, turning on his lackeys. "You were only supposed to bring me the goods." He looked over his shoulder for an instant. "Get rid of her."

Martin paled.

Mrs. Danvers was made of far sterner stuff. "You can do your own dirty work, Mr. Green. We have done everything you've asked and more. This is the end of it. The emeralds more than repay any debt we owe you."

The weaselly wheeler-dealer snarled. "I say when it's over, Mrs. Danvers. Maybe you think you can embezzle household money from Carlotta and the prince, and get away with it, but I know about you." He grinned. It was a horrible grin. "I know all about you *and* your son."

The housekeeper's eyes flared with savage rage. "You...you..."

Crispy raised a pudgy finger and wagged it at her. "Tut-tut." Then he quickly turned his head in the direction of the storeroom door and muttered, "What the devil's going on around here?"

The sound of drunken singing was coming from the other side of the room.

There once was a young lady from Bath,
Who many believed to be daft.
She loved making the gentlemen laugh,
By hitching up her skirts whenever they...

"Oh, I do beg your pardon," slurred Trout as he staggered into their midst, reeking of alcohol. "I did not realize—" he burped loudly in Crispy Green's face "—that there were ladies present."

Samantha's mouth fell open. She couldn't believe her eyes. Trout was in a disgraceful state. He was drunk. His hair was disheveled. His clothing was stained and torn. He was wearing only his right shoe; apparently he had lost the left. He had a bottle of liquor in one hand and some kind of odd stick clutched in the other.

He began to dance a little jig and sing softly under his breath. Then he glanced up with red-rimmed eyes. "Would anyone care to have this dance? Mrs. Danvers? Professor Wainwright? Oh dear, you seem tied up at the moment, Professor." He giggled. "Another time, perhaps?"

Crispy Green exploded into ugly language. "What in the hell is the fool up to?"

"That would seem obvious," Mrs. Danvers said with the full force of her disapproval. "Trout has been drinking like a fish."

The butler burped loudly again and held up the stick in his hand. "Cricket, anyone?"

The skin around Crispy Green's mouth grew taut. "I've never known Trout to touch a drop of alcohol."

"Neither have I," piped up Martin timidly.

"There's a first time for everyone and everything," stated Mrs. Danvers.

With that, the Englishman began to sing even louder and dance even more wildly, drowning out the housekeeper, her son, even the man in charge.

Suddenly, just at the edge of her peripheral vision, Samantha saw something move.

Someone else was in the storeroom. Someone was behind the shelves filled with antiquities. Someone was making his way skillfully, silently, stealthily, toward their group.

It could only be one person, of course: Jonathan.

Samantha managed not to look in his direction. The last thing she wanted to do was give away his presence to Crispy Green and his henchmen. She sank her teeth into her bottom lip to keep herself from crying out his name. Her heart was beating faster and faster.

She sensed that Crispy was getting suspicious and she knew she had to do something.

Samantha opened her mouth and began to sing along with Trout. "'There once was a young lady from Bath. Who many believed to be daft...'"

The man's face turned bright red with indignation. "What in the bloody hell is going on here?"

The singing stopped abruptly.

Jonathan stepped up behind Crispy and positioned his gun point-blank at the toad's head. "That is for me to know, Green, and for you to find out."

"Hazard!"

"Right the first time."

"You bastard, I knew you were going to be trouble from the start!"

"You were right. You should have listened to your instincts," Jonathan said sardonically.

Mrs. Danvers and Martin made a move to leave.

"Not so fast, you two," commanded a very sober Trout as he brandished his cricket bat in their faces. "There is no sense in trying to escape," he informed the villainous group. "I have already telephoned the police, and awakened Madam and the prince. The gig is up!"

"I thought you were wonderful, Trout," Samantha exclaimed, and she meant it.

"Thank you, Professor." It was several hours later and he was serving coffee, medicinally laced with brandy. "But I still blame myself."

"How could you possibly be to blame? You had no idea Crispy Green was a criminal, that he had lost huge sums of money and was blackmailing your staff in order to recover some of his losses."

The Englishman sighed and shook his head. "Mrs. Danvers and Martin were my responsibility. It was my business to realize something was wrong. If nothing else, I should have *sensed* it." He sighed again. "I shall never forgive myself."

"But you must," Samantha pleaded. "Mustn't he, Jonathan?" she said, turning to her ally for backup.

"I couldn't have done it tonight without you, Trout. You were the front man who put Crispy off the scent so I could slip in behind enemy lines. It was a two-man job. You did your part brilliantly."

"I appreciate your words of encouragement and goodwill, but I must tender my resignation immediately." The Englishman was adamant.

Samantha took a sip of her coffee and said thoughtfully, "After this unfortunate affair, Carlotta and the prince will need you more than ever. I can't imagine how they will manage if you desert them."

"Desert them?"

Jonathan patted him on the shoulder. "You can't just up and leave your post, old chap."

"But...but I was grooming Martin to take my place one day," he confessed.

"We all make mistakes about people," Samantha declared. "You can't always judge a book by its cover." Then she added, "You must stay, and hire new staff."

There was a fire in his eyes. "This time I'm going to insist we have those newfangled security checks run on anyone who applies for employment," Trout stated.

"I believe I can help you there," volunteered Jonathan.

Trout shook his hand. "I had a feeling you were a gentleman of many talents, sir."

If Trout only knew *how* many talents, Samantha reflected as she rose from her chair, stretched her arms over her head and announced in a sleepy voice, "I've had quite enough excitement for one night. I am going to bed."

Jonathan stood and said politely, "May I escort you to your room, Professor?"

"Thank you. That would be very kind, Mr. Hazard."

"I didn't volunteer to be kind," he admitted once they were alone.

Samantha let her eyes go wide with innocent surprise. "Really? Then why did you volunteer?"

Jonathan looked down at her and grinned. "You're wearing my shirt, lady."

Fifteen

———

"I thought Carlotta was particularly fetching in the hat she wore while being interviewed by the police," Samantha mentioned as they strolled toward the Egyptian wing.

"Fetching?" Jonathan remarked dryly. "It looked good enough to eat."

She gave a tired laugh. "That no doubt explains the hungry expression I saw on the faces of one or two of the detectives."

"What do you expect if you're going to display a bowl of lifelike exotic fruit on your head?"

Samantha stifled a yawn. "Carlotta is really very sweet. Do you know she has given me the green silk dress to take home?"

"Now, *that* is a delicious thought," Jonathan murmured, slipping his arm around her waist.

She sighed and leaned her head against his strong shoulder. "I was more than a little surprised when Henry asked us to call him Henry."

"Yup, no more Prince Henri this, or Prince Henri that."

"Only to outsiders."

"I guess that means we aren't outsiders anymore." Jonathan gave her a quick sideways glance. "I've always preferred to be an insider."

Samantha groaned. "How can you make sexual innuendos at a time like this?"

He shrugged. "A time like *what?*"

"I'm exhausted," she confessed. "I stayed up most of the night making love with you. I got maybe five minutes of sleep. I was abducted by a band of crazed criminals—"

He quirked a dark eyebrow. "Crazed criminals?"

"Okay, a nasty bunch of embezzlers and lowlifes, not to mention potential murderers," Samantha said with a certain grim amusement. "I was scared out of my wits that you would do something heroic and get killed trying to save me, or, at the least, seriously damage important parts of your anatomy."

"What important parts?"

"I don't think this is the time or the place to go into that."

"Why not?"

She gave him a long, measuring look. "You might get ideas."

"Ideas?"

She nodded. "Yes. Ideas."

Jonathan seemed perfectly willing to play dumb. "What kind of ideas?"

Samantha sighed. "The kind I'm too tired to do anything about. The kind I would say an emphatic N-O to. The kind I would have to nip in the bud."

He grinned. "Nip in the bud? That brings a pretty picture to mind."

Samantha looked at him like he was crazy. "Don't you need any sleep?"

"Sure. Everybody needs some sleep."

"Aren't you tired?"

She saw a flash of white teeth. "Pumped up with adrenaline is more like it."

"Well, I don't care what you're pumped with—or what's pumped up, for that matter—I am going to bed and I am going to sleep, and I intend to sleep for as long as I like."

"Hey," Jonathan said with a casual gesture, "feel free."

"Thank you." Samantha opened the door to the Cleopatra Suite, and when the man behind her made to follow her inside, she put out a hand and stopped him. "I will sleep in *my* bedroom. And you will do whatever it is you intend to do in *your* bedroom."

His handsome face fell for a moment. Then he seemed to cheer up. "In case you hadn't noticed, Professor, it's morning. The sun is shining. The birds are singing. The bad guys are in jail, and all is right with the world."

"It will be once I get eight hours of sleep," Samantha stated with no sense of humor. "See you this afternoon, Mr. Hazard. Or better yet, this evening." She glanced down at the chambray shirt she was wearing. "And don't worry, I'll take good care of your shirt."

Jonathan leaned his shoulder against the doorframe and said with a baiting smile. "Are you going to have my shirt washed and ironed?"

"I intend to sleep in it first." She shut the door, then called to him. "Good night, Jonathan."

"Good morning, Sam, honey."

When Samantha awoke, it was evening. There was a slight chill in the air and the sun was gone, leaving behind only a trace of its former brilliant light.

She turned over and looked up at the glassy, lifelike eyes of the carved ram's head staring fixedly down at her from atop the bedpost.

It had been a strange week and a half.

In many ways she was not at all the same woman who had left Chicago ten days ago to come to Fontainebleau to examine and catalog Archibald McDonnell's famed collection. That woman had been concerned only with her career as an Egyptologist. That woman had been unsure of her attractiveness as a female. That woman had trusted only her intellect, and not her emotions.

That woman had been uncomfortable with men. Men under the age of fifty.

Men like Jonathan Hazard.

Jonathan still frightened her, but not in the way he had in the beginning. At first, she had been half-afraid he would make a pass at her. The kind of inconsequential sexual pass some men tried with any presentable female who happened along.

Now she only feared that Jonathan might not be attracted to her with the same intensity, the same depth of feeling with which she found herself attracted to him.

She was in love.

"Ohmigod!" Samantha's hand flew to her mouth. Tears sprang out of nowhere and ran down her cheeks.

She was in love with Jonathan Hazard!

How could it be? When had it happened? Only a few short hours ago—it seemed like days, like weeks, like months—she had literally laughed in his face when he had suggested that they were in love.

"I can't be in love with you and you certainly can't be in love with me," she had informed him unconditionally.

She remembered her exact thoughts. They couldn't be in love with each other. The notion was ridiculous. It was crazy. It was insane. It was stupid.

"So call me stupid," Samantha muttered to herself as she lay in the big bed and stared at the ceiling.

Her gaze lowered to the ancient gold pyramid sitting on the table. She had been so wrapped up in the idea of a secret place, a hiding place, that she had not once stopped to consider that the greatest hiding place was the human heart.

Samantha was still trying to absorb this incredible piece of information when a soft knock came on her wall.

"Come in!" she called out as she pushed herself up onto her elbows.

The secret door opened and Jonathan walked into the Cleopatra Suite. He was showered, shaved, dressed in a clean pair of jeans and a shirt identical to the one she was wearing.

"Good evening!" Jonathan said as he bent over and dropped a kiss on her mouth. "Ah, no 'morning breath,'" he noted with a sly grin as he deposited himself in the chair beside her bed.

"Are you always going to be this cheerful?" she asked with a dubious look.

"Always."

"Then there will have to be some basic rules, a few simple guidelines," she told him.

"A few simple guidelines," he echoed.

"I need my sleep."

"You need your sleep."

"I do not like to talk out loud until I have had at least two cups of strong, black coffee."

"Two cups of strong, black coffee."

"I cannot tolerate singing in the shower until after ten A.M., and only then if you can carry a tune and sing on key."

Jonathan sat back, crossed one long, muscular leg over the other and intertwined his fingers. "Are you trying to tell me in your own inimitable way, Professor, that you are not a morning person?"

"Brilliant deduction, Sherlock," she muttered, and pushed herself up farther in the bed.

"Is there anything else I should know?" he asked with a typically sardonic expression on his mouth, but Samantha noticed that his eyes were serious.

"I'll return your shirt as soon as I can have it washed and ironed," she vowed.

"Honey, you can keep the damned shirt. As a matter of fact, you can have my pants, too, if you need them." Jonathan stood up and began to unzip the front of his jeans.

"That won't be necessary," she quickly assured him. "But I appreciate the offer and I will keep it in mind."

"See that you do," he said. "Oh, I believe these are yours." He tossed the pouch of emeralds onto the bed.

Samantha sighed. "Not mine. They belong to the Kemet Museum now, part of a permanent exhibit that will be displayed one day, thanks to Archibald McDonnell."

"You made your once-in-a-lifetime find, didn't you?"

She glanced down at the pouch of precious stones. "Yes, I did."

But they weren't talking about the same kind of once-in-a-lifetime find. *Jonathan* was her once-in-a-lifetime, Samantha realized.

Would she have the guts to tell him? Would she be brave enough to come right out and say "I love you" to the man? Or, in the end, would she chicken out?

She sat up a little straighter and looked him right in the eye, even though he towered over her. "I think there are several basic rules and simple guidelines we failed to mention."

That got Jonathan's attention. He slowly sank onto the edge of the mattress. His expression was wary. "Really?"

Samantha nodded. "To begin with, no dogs. At least not Pekingese."

She could see the tension begin to ease from the man's broad shoulders.

"I think I can safely speak for both of us when I say that Trigger and I approve," he said.

"Second, we will never hire a housekeeper named Mrs. Danvers, no matter how good her references are."

Jonathan slapped his thigh. "Done!"

She was feeling almost lighthearted. "We will only speak French when we are actually in France."

"But, *mon chère*—" he shrugged and managed a fairly good impression of Maurice Chevalier "—what if I wish to whisper the sweet nothings in your ear? What do I do then?"

She pretended to think about it for half a minute. "Oh, all right, you can whisper sweet nothings in French. But only sweet nothings."

Jonathan was suddenly serious. "What are you trying to tell me, Samantha?"

She took a deep, fortifying breath and let it out again. "I'm trying to tell you that I love you."

He appeared stunned. "You love me."

"In fact, I'm proposing."

Jonathan hadn't moved a muscle. Indeed, he seemed incapable of moving anything but his lips, and even his lips weren't working properly. "Proposing *what?*"

"Marriage."

Jonathan Michelangelo Hazard had waited a lifetime for the right woman to say the right words to him, and now that she had, all he could do was sit there and stare at her like an idiot.

Samantha loved him. She wanted to marry him. In fact, she had just proposed.

Her face was beginning to change from ivory to pink. He had better say something quick or she would turn bright red and take it all back.

"I accept," he blurted out.

Samantha sat upright in the big bed, folded her arms under her breasts and glared at him. "That isn't what you're supposed to say."

He was baffled. "It isn't?"

"No, you're supposed to take me in your arms and declare your undying devotion. Then you should cover my face, my hands, even my feet with kisses, all the while declaring that you can't live without me, that you have waited your whole life for me, that I am the right woman for you, that I am the only woman for you. It would be appropriate to conclude with something like you're lucky I'm in love with you because you are hopelessly and madly in love with me."

Jonathan reached for her and declared, "I *can't* live without you. I *have* waited my whole life for you. You *are* the one and only woman for me. And I am damned lucky you love me, Professor, because I'm wildly, madly and hopelessly in love with you."

"That's better," she sniffed.

"Now shut up and kiss me, Sam."

"Why should I?"

"Because I'll die if I have to wait another second to feel your sweet mouth under mine," he vowed.

Jonathan kissed her until he was crazy and she was dizzy. He had one hand on the buttons of the shirt he was wearing, and the other on the buttons of the twin Samantha had slept in. He had never tried to unbutton two shirts at once—it took all of his concentration and coordination and then some—while he was kissing the woman he was going to make his wife.

His wife.

He liked the sound of it. No, he *loved* the sound of it.

He raised his head for a moment and tried it out. "Mr. and Professor Samantha Hazard." He shook his head. "Professor and Mr. Jonathan Hazard."

Samantha laughed against his mouth. "Mr. and Mrs. Jonathan Hazard when I'm not at the office."

He nodded. "The same for me. Mr. and Mrs. Jonathan Hazard when I'm not at the office."

She gazed up at him as he tossed both shirts onto the floor. "I've waited my whole life for you, haven't I?"

"Yup. Smart woman," he mumbled, concentrating on the spot behind her ear, the hollow at the base of her throat, the soft swell of her breasts. "And I've waited my whole life for you."

"Smart man," she declared, her hands finding the button at his waistband.

By the time Samantha managed to release him from the constraints of his jeans, he was fully hard and eagerly sprang into her awaiting palms. Her touch was cool, but it only made him hotter and hotter. Jonathan heard a low groan of pure masculine pleasure and realized it was him.

"We are crazy, aren't we?" Samantha murmured as her lips followed the erotic trail first blazed by her fingertips.

"Yes."

"We are insane," she added, finding him with her lips, her teeth, her tongue.

She was driving him insane. He was quickly and quietly and completely going out of his mind.

"I know one thing," he gasped as he pulled her up his body and settled her hips astride his. "We love each other."

He cupped her breasts, then used his thumbs as an erotic device to flick back and forth across her nipples until they became two tight buds.

He urged her closer and closer to his mouth. He drew her in deeper and stronger, and suckled her. He licked at her with the tip of his tongue and nipped her softly with his teeth until she cried out his name.

"We love what we do to each other, as well," she admitted as she moved rhythmically above him. "Can we make love all night long, Jonathan?"

"We can try, sweetheart," he said through his teeth as he drove into her sweet body again and again. "We can damn well try."

It was sometime later—frankly Jonathan Hazard had no idea how much later and he didn't particularly care—that Samantha nuzzled his neck and said, "I don't think I ever thanked you for saving my life."

"It isn't necessary to thank me."

She kissed his cheek. "Thank you, anyway."

"You're welcome."

She kissed his jaw. "Thank you."

"It was nothing."

She kissed his ear, touching the tip of her tongue to the sensitive skin and nipping the lobe with her teeth. "Thank you."

His heart rate was accelerating. "Happy to be of service, ma'am."

She nuzzled his neck and throat. "Thank you, sir."

Jonathan found it was becoming harder and harder to breathe. And that wasn't the only thing becoming harder. "Anytime," he managed.

Samantha dropped a whole slew of kisses on his chest and declared, "You were wonderful."

"Glad . . . you think so."

She pressed her mouth to the tensed muscles of his abdomen and murmured, "I don't know what I would have done if you hadn't come to my rescue."

Who was going to come to *his* rescue? Jonathan wondered. He *had* created a monster. The professor was driving him certifiably insane.

"Samantha—?"

She raised her head and looked at him. "Yes, darling?"

"You don't have to keep thanking me."

"But I want to."

"It isn't necessary."

"I think it is. After all, you saved my life." She frowned. "Come to think of it. You once saved Uncle George's life, too, didn't you?"

"The circumstances were vastly different, believe me," Jonathan said with a touch of irony.

"Perhaps." She chewed on her bottom lip for a moment. "Tell me something."

"Anything."

"That first day you came to my office at the Kemet Museum, I called Uncle George on the telephone and you said something that has puzzled me ever since."

Jonathan combed his hands through her silky hair as it lay draped across his body. "What?"

"You said, 'Tell George I owe him another one.'"

Jonathan smiled. "I remember."

Samantha raised her head and looked at him with eyes filled with love. "Another *what*?"

"Favor."

She frowned. "That's it? A favor?"

He shrugged. "Yup. It was kind of a joke. He owed me, you see."

Now, of course, he really did owe that wily George

Huxley a favor, Jonathan realized as he gathered the beautiful woman in his arms.

But somehow he didn't mind...

*   *   *   *   *

Look for the next instalment of Hazards Inc.,
The Pirate Princess.
Coming in June from Silhouette Desire.

Fifty red-blooded, white-hot, true-blue hunks
from every State in the Union!

Look for MEN MADE IN AMERICA! Written by some
of our most popular authors, these stories feature fifty
of the strongest, sexiest men, each from a different state
in the union!

Two titles available every other month at your favorite
retail outlet.

In April, look for:

LOVE BY PROXY by Diana Palmer (Illinois)
POSSIBLES by Lass Small (Indiana)

In May, look for:

KISS YESTERDAY GOODBYE by Leigh Michaels (Iowa)
A TIME TO KEEP by Curtiss Ann Matlock (Kansas)

You won't be able to resist MEN MADE IN AMERICA!

SILHOUETTE® Desire®

"She's a no-good floozy out to ruin my son's name!"
—Lucy Dooley's ex-mother-in-law

OUTER BANKS

LUCY AND THE STONE
by Dixie Browning

When May's *Man of the Month,* Stone McCloud, was sent to North Carolina's Outer Banks to keep Lucy in line, he couldn't find a floozy anywhere on Coronoke Island. There was only a very *sweet* Lucy. Was she trying to wrap him around her ringless finger—and then do him in?

Don't miss LUCY AND THE STONE by Dixie Browning, available in May from Silhouette Desire.

INDULGE A LITTLE 6947 SWEEPSTAKES
NO PURCHASE NECESSARY

HERE'S HOW THE SWEEPSTAKES WORKS:

The Harlequin Reader Service shipments for January, February and March 1994 will contain, respectively, coupons for entry into three prize drawings: a trip for two to San Francisco, an Alaskan cruise for two and a trip for two to Hawaii. To be eligible for any drawing using an Entry Coupon, simply complete and mail according to directions.

There is no obligation to continue as a Reader Service subscriber to enter and be eligible for any prize drawing. You may also enter any drawing by hand printing your name and address on a 3" x 5" card and the destination of the prize you wish that entry to be considered for (i.e., San Francisco trip, Alaskan cruise or Hawaiian trip). Send your 3" x 5" entries to: Indulge a Little 6947 Sweepstakes, c/o Prize Destination you wish that entry to be considered for, P.O. Box 1315, Buffalo, NY 14269-1315, U.S.A. or Indulge a Little 6947 Sweepstakes, P.O. Box 610, Fort Erie, Ontario L2A 5X3, Canada.

To be eligible for the San Francisco trip, entries must be received by 4/30/94; for the Alaskan cruise, 5/31/94; and the Hawaiian trip, 6/30/94. No responsibility is assumed for lost, late or misdirected mail. Sweepstakes open to residents of the U.S. (except Puerto Rico) and Canada, 18 years of age or older. All applicable laws and regulations apply. Sweepstakes void wherever prohibited.

For a copy of the Official Rules, send a self-addressed, stamped envelope (WA residents need not affix return postage) to: Indulge a Little 6947 Rules, P.O. Box 4631, Blair, NE 68009, U.S.A.

INDR93

INDULGE A LITTLE 6947 SWEEPSTAKES
NO PURCHASE NECESSARY

HERE'S HOW THE SWEEPSTAKES WORKS:

The Harlequin Reader Service shipments for January, February and March 1994 will contain, respectively, coupons for entry into three prize drawings: a trip for two to San Francisco, an Alaskan cruise for two and a trip for two to Hawaii. To be eligible for any drawing using an Entry Coupon, simply complete and mail according to directions.

There is no obligation to continue as a Reader Service subscriber to enter and be eligible for any prize drawing. You may also enter any drawing by hand printing your name and address on a 3" x 5" card and the destination of the prize you wish that entry to be considered for (i.e., San Francisco trip, Alaskan cruise or Hawaiian trip). Send your 3" x 5" entries to: Indulge a Little 6947 Sweepstakes, c/o Prize Destination you wish that entry to be considered for, P.O. Box 1315, Buffalo, NY 14269-1315, U.S.A. or Indulge a Little 6947 Sweepstakes, P.O. Box 610, Fort Erie, Ontario L2A 5X3, Canada.

To be eligible for the San Francisco trip, entries must be received by 4/30/94; for the Alaskan cruise, 5/31/94; and the Hawaiian trip, 6/30/94. No responsibility is assumed for lost, late or misdirected mail. Sweepstakes open to residents of the U.S. (except Puerto Rico) and Canada, 18 years of age or older. All applicable laws and regulations apply. Sweepstakes void wherever prohibited.

For a copy of the Official Rules, send a self-addressed, stamped envelope (WA residents need not affix return postage) to: Indulge a Little 6947 Rules, P.O. Box 4631, Blair, NE 68009, U.S.A.

INDR93

INDULGE A LITTLE
SWEEPSTAKES

OFFICIAL ENTRY COUPON

This entry must be received by: APRIL 30, 1994
This month's winner will be notified by: MAY 15, 1994
Trip must be taken between: JUNE 30, 1994-JUNE 30, 1995

YES, I want to win the San Francisco vacation for two. I understand that the prize includes round-trip airfare, first-class hotel, rental car and pocket money as revealed on the "wallet" scratch-off card.

Name_____

Address _____ Apt. _____

City_____

State/Prov._____ Zip/Postal Code_____

Daytime phone number_____
                          (Area Code)

Account #_____

Return entries with invoice in envelope provided. Each book in this shipment has two entry coupons—and the more coupons you enter, the better your chances of winning!
© 1993 HARLEQUIN ENTERPRISES LTD.   MONTH1

INDULGE A LITTLE
SWEEPSTAKES

OFFICIAL ENTRY COUPON

This entry must be received by: APRIL 30, 1994
This month's winner will be notified by: MAY 15, 1994
Trip must be taken between: JUNE 30, 1994-JUNE 30, 1995

YES, I want to win the San Francisco vacation for two. I understand that the prize includes round-trip airfare, first-class hotel, rental car and pocket money as revealed on the "wallet" scratch-off card.

Name_____

Address _____ Apt. _____

City_____

State/Prov._____ Zip/Postal Code_____

Daytime phone number_____
                          (Area Code)

Account #_____

Return entries with invoice in envelope provided. Each book in this shipment has two entry coupons—and the more coupons you enter, the better your chances of winning!
© 1993 HARLEQUIN ENTERPRISES LTD.   MONTH1